On hands, on knees, slowly at first, then more quickly, he entered the tunnel. It was apparently a tunnel which would give forth into the mercury lake outside. In his mind's eye, he could see Gull Norse, already at work prying open the jets, getting ready to take off. Suddenly the full meaning of what had happened struck him. He went faster, as fast as his horrified thoughts.

And the unexpected happened. . . .

—From "The Bottled Men"

Waldman

THE MEN
AND THE MIRROR

by
Ross Rocklynne

ace books
A Division of Charter Communications Inc.
1120 Avenue of the Americas
New York, N.Y. 10036

THE MEN AND THE MIRROR

Copyright © 1973, by Ross L. Rocklin

An Ace Book. All Rights Reserved.

ACKNOWLEDGMENTS:

"At the Center of Gravity," from *Astounding Stories,* June, 1936; copyright © 1936 by Street & Smith, Inc.

"Jupiter Trap," from *Astounding Stories,* August 1937; copyright © 1937 by Street & Smith, Inc.

"The Men and the Mirror," from *Astounding Science-Fiction,* July, 1938; copyright © 1938 by Street & Smith, Inc.

Robert D. Swisher letter from *Astounding Stories,* November, 1938; copyright © 1938 by Street and Smith, Inc.

"They Fly So High," from *Amazing Stories,* June, 1952; copyright © 1952 by Ziff-Davis Publishing Co., Inc.

"The Bottled Men," from *Astounding Science-Fiction,* June, 1946; copyright © 1946 by Street & Smith, Inc.

"And Then There Was One," from *Astounding Science-Fiction,* February, 1940; copyright © 1940 by Street & Smith, Inc.; copyright © 1968 by Ross L. Rocklin.

AUTHOR'S DEDICATION:

To my mother, who has fun with words too.

First Ace printing: February, 1973

Printed in U.S.A.

CONTENTS

AT THE CENTER OF GRAVITY 10

JUPITER TRAP 31

THE MEN AND THE MIRROR 58

THEY FLY SO HIGH 109

THE BOTTLED MEN 127

INTRODUCTION

Here are six stories related in two ways. One of these ways is by a plot pattern which is fairly common and, indeed, fairly uncomplicated—the plot pattern of the hunter and the hunted, or, if you will, cops 'n' robbers. The second way they are related is by the science fiction device called the "scientific idea."

If there is a definition of science fiction of the earlier days, or perhaps even of the latter days, which stands a chance of holding up better than others, it is that a science fiction story is a set of made-up events built around and motivated by a novel scientific idea.

Early science fiction most often was constructed around the novel scientific idea. It gave the author his plot development and his characters. The story of Icarus grew from a highly original idea of a scientific nature. H.G. Wells's plots or characters are barely remembered, though his scientific ideas became basic to much of later science fiction. If any of Verne's characters are remembered, such as Captain Nemo, it is only against the backdrop of that pearl of an idea, the underseas ship, or submarine.

In 1926, in the then-new *Amazing Stories,* other such pearls, the first of hundreds, and then of thousands, were to be conceived by new writers scratching around with rough-cut particles culled from mostly informal scientific educations. Many of the early names are memorable. Using a truly startling scientific idea, Charles Cloukey was one of the first writers to send an artificial satellite around the moon. The satellite was a bullet which the villain fired from a standing position on the lunar surface. Upon completion of its first orbit, the bullet lodged in the victim's back. The plot is standard "biter-bit," and you can make up your own. The scientific idea was the important ingredient.

Few historians or apologists within the field of science fiction have pointed out that science fiction often was labeled "'stories of pseudo-science." Early in the days of *Amazing Stories*, Hugo Gernsback realized he would have to relent his strictures calling for faultless science, otherwise few stories would stand the test of publication. We see something of this at work in *Boomerang 'Round the Moon*, by David H. Keller, M.D. In my opinion, the idea was a charming one and therefore it seemed forgiveable; but aerodynamically the story was unstable. Similarly, Bob Olsen cut through our common sense (we were willing he did so) by retrieving a scissors left in a patient by moving through the fourth dimension to the cross-section of space and time containing it. Miles J. Breuer, M.D., also wrote an impossible story about dimensional transit. It was called *The Gostak and the Doshes*. The semantics of the key concept, that is, "The gostak diskims the doshes," was quite fascinating. The questions we naturally ask have to do with the meaning of the three strange words. The answers are astonishing. A gostak is that which acts on a dosh by diskimming it. A dosh is obviously that which is diskimmed. The meaning of diskim now becomes apparent! These stories were too good to turn down because the authors bent the science; indeed, the stories were good because of pseudo-science.

Though there was this permissiveness in stretching science, readers (and the reading-writers as well) were quick to pounce on an author who became too lackadaisical. Their letters to the discussions columns of the magazines were often critical—but forgiving: in spite of the errors, the reader might indicate a given story was the best in the book. When I started writing science fiction, I was quite fearful of two things. One was my writing ability, and one was reader reaction to my science.

I decided that if I didn't know how to write as well as the better writers, I had better bolster my stories with good scientific backbones so that the editors could not help but buy them, and the readers could not find fault with them. How did this scheme work out? So-so. I liked my own ideas, and this in turn lent an enthusiasm to my writing which got it past the editors. I did not entirely avoid reader reaction of the kind I was afraid of, however, for in spite of everything errors crept in. I was forgiven! Readers liked my "problem stories," as they were called, and this became the kind of scientific idea I liked to build stories around, if I could.

This group of six stories, culled from a stretch of years between 1936 and 1952, does not represent all of the problem stories I wrote, but they are related in a special way beyond that: The first three stories are connected as a series involving two characters, a cop and a robber. Numbers four and five *should* have belonged to the same series—and really do—except that circumstances impelled me to change the names, backgrounds, and personalities of the male protagonists. The sixth story departs from the cops 'n' robbers formula of the first five, but not too much. It is included because it lets you know why the premise of the first story is—*shudder*—scientifically incorrect.

Problems, problems. . . .

Six of them.

—Ross Rocklynne
Los Angeles, California

AT THE CENTER OF GRAVITY
(*Astounding Stories*, June 1936)

The following story was written in a year when most science fiction spaceships were cigar-shaped. Mine were no exceptions. In these chemically-powered rocket ships we moved about the solar system at astonishing speeds. Trips to distant planets might take hours, or days, perhaps a week, maybe a month to Pluto. There might be a reference to the "frightful distances" between planets, but for story purposes we preferred to move pretty fast. In this story we make use of a very handy mythical planet called Vulcan: I've used it four or five times in different yarns. In this story, the planet is hollow. Question: What is wrong with the basic story idea? Turn to the last of the six stories, *And Then There Was One,* to find out.

The two of them, Lieutenant Jack Colbie and Edward Deverel, hung suspended without visible support in a space which, had it not been for the beam of light thrown by the lieutenant on his captured prisoner, would have been quite dark.

Jack Colbie was a direct social opposite of the other man. And Jack Colbie, of the Interplanetary Police Force, was widely known as a relentless tracker of criminals. Edward Deverel was the criminal, at the present instant, and Colbie had caught up with him. The chase had started in Deverel's own domain, the domain of his piratical activities—the red deserts of Mars, and the broad canals that cut through them.

Both were clad in the tough, insulated, smoothly curving suits that man must wear in space. The transparent helmets afforded external vision, and now Deverel was looking through his at Colbie insolently. But, since the scant illumination Colbie received came from the reflection of the beam he held on his prisoner, Deverel saw him as a gray shadow on the complete darkness stretching away behind.

"Well?" he inquired, with a disdainful flash of his white teeth, whiter still in the light of the beam.

"Well, nothing. Don't look so peeved. What else did you expect? You knew I'd catch up with you. I've got to maintain an unbroken record."

Deverel shrugged his shoulders. They could just be seen through his helmet. "Precedent doesn't prove anything."

"Oh, I suppose not. Forget it." Colbie studied the corsair's face. Deverel was good-looking, undoubtedly—better-looking than Colbie, certainly, who had a ravaged profile and a long jaw.

Deverel's nose was straight; he possessed attractive, but almost bitterly formed, lips; his eyes were blue, and the constant inner deviltry of his nature burned in their depths.

"Let's forget you're my prisoner. Let's talk a while. I'm curious as to why you landed on Vulcan."

"Why?" Deverel laughed. "Did you want me to take a dive into the Sun?

"Well, you were crowding me. I had to leave Mars, of course, when my band of canal marauders succumbed before Jack Colbie and his police. You chased me, Colbie, as I've never before been chased in this incarnation. I was going to land on Earth—I could have found a hideout—but you headed me off. So I tried Venus. Same thing. So what was left but Vulcan? Mercury was fooling around somewhere on the other side of the Sun.

"Oh, I guess I was a fool to land, since I knew that was what you wanted me to do. But you know what empty space and stars do to a man. The bigness of things gives him a colossal inferiority complex, and it puts him in the mood for anything. What I mean is, a man doesn't care. I was feeling something of that, and besides, I was tired of running, of being chased. That's why I landed on Vulcan, when I knew there wasn't a hiding place on its smooth surface."

"And, as it turned out," Colbie put in, "there was a hiding place. Only, I found you."

"And what good's it going to do you?" Deverel laughed in genuine amusement. "I've just been checking, and, according to the oxygen gauge, I won't live for twenty-four hours. I'll bet a binary your tank is in the same condition. There isn't any way of escape.

"Well," he went on in a dreamy fashion, "I suppose I've been skid-rayed. Skid-rayed by a cop at last. I always knew it would happen, though. That last stunt of breaking up the empress' canal excursion party was what got the I. P. after me."

He craned his eyes at Colbie. "But things have a habit of checking to zero. You're what you are, I'm what I am, and we're going to die. But who had the most kick out of it? Did you like to put men in prison? I wonder. But me! It was fun to slip the rings off the fat fingers of the empress!"

There was a shrug in Colbie's voice. "Maybe it was. Let's leave philosophy out of it. How did you happen to find the hole?"

"Well, I didn't look for it. Vulcan's never been considered worth a detailed investigation, and so nobody knew the startling facts about the little planet.

"I saw the hole on a jump of ten miles across the surface, revealed by starlight. As much as I remember, it was about forty feet across, and on the night side, with the day side only seventy or so miles away. Anyway, I saw it, and I knew you were hopping after me somewhere on the night side, and I didn't give a damn anymore, which, added to plain curiosity, made me jump in. The hole," said Deverel whimsically, "was deep, and I fell for hours. I suppose you knew I was down here, when you found the hole, eh?"

"After I had started falling," Colbie said. "I'd looked everywhere on the night side and hadn't found you. The day side was of course too hot. I was going back to the two ships. Wherever you were, you wouldn't escape the planet. Then I fell in, from a long jump. I couldn't avoid it.

"About seven hours down," he continued, "I began to suspect the truth—that Vulcan is as hollow as a bubble, probably is one, the result of a huge, internal explosion, just before it cooled, ages ago. Some other explosion pushed a hole through the crust.

"At first I thought I'd stop when even with the inner surface. Second thought showed otherwise. If the planet was actually hollow, I'd drop to the center, at a steadily decreasing speed. The law of gravitation says that every particle of matter in the universe attracts every other particle with a force that is directly proportional to the product of their masses, and inversely proportional to the square of the distance between their centers.

"Of course, Vulcan being a sphere, there was lateral attraction as well as vertical. The gravitational force pulling me away from center was less than that pulling me toward it, but as I went along they tended to become

13

equal to each other, until, here at the center of gravity, the forces of gravity neutralize. For every pull from one direction there's another of equal force from the opposite direction.

"We fell to Vulcan's center in a straight line, but on Earth, if it were hollow, we wouldn't. Weight manifests itself in a line somewhat removed from the center of gravity, because of centrifugal force on the Earth's surface. You'd fall in a spiral path. But Vulcan doesn't rotate."

Their two bodies, having tendencies to drift to the exact center of Vulcan, were touching. Colbie pushed Deverel away by raising his knee.

"You've remarked a few times that my taking you prisoner was a joke," remarked Colbie. "What makes you think so?"

"Because there's no way of escape," said Deverel calmly. "Maybe you think so, too, and don't know it. Else you'd have put me in handcuffs, in addition to taking my projector.

"Here's the situation! Vulcan is hollow. I'm sure there's only one outlet. We're at the center. Now how are we going to reach the outlet? It's a riddle, and I know your first guess."

"All right, I'll make it! How about reaction? I've got a hundred rounds for my projector, and—you've got at least fifty on your belt."

"First guess wrong." Deverel mockingly shook his head. "I've thought of reaction—the only thought, incidentally. I was here hours before you were, and I was able to pick the thing to pieces.

"No matter which way you take it, it won't work. Worse than that, it's suicide. Consider. Vulcan is eight hundred and ninety miles in diameter, and hollow. Probably the crust is a hundred miles in thickness—a thinner one would crack up under the attraction of the Sun. That would give us three hundred and forty-five miles to travel by reaction—to the inner surface. Once we got there, our simple problem would be to find the hole, which is anywhere on the inner surface, quite a considerable area. But probably we wouldn't even get there, because we wouldn't know whether we were going toward the day side or the night side. Or we might execute circles.

"But let's say we do reach the inner surface. How would we stay there? By hanging onto jutting rocks? Then what if we lost our holds? We'd drop back to center. Then, too, the inner surface is probably a hotbed of chemical action. Where else would these gases come from?" He swept his arm through a short arc, producing a swishing whine by way of illustration.

"It wouldn't be fun to grab hold of smoking-hot spur of basalt, even though your doxite gloves are nearly perfect nonconductors.

"Don't think I'm afraid of taking a chance," he hastened to add. "But this isn't even a chance. It's simply quicker death. We'd drop back, I'll bet a binary, and there'd be a batch of explosive shells waiting for us. They wouldn't travel all the way to the surface, and the least contact with anything solid would set them off. And they'd drop back to center."

Colbie listened him out, and suddenly snapped off his flashlight. "You picked the flaws in the tube," he said heavily. "But—"

"If it gets to that point," Deverel agreed with the unvoiced thought, "we'll try reaction. Or else, if we can discover some means beside reaction to get to the surface, we'll do that. But—"

There was infinite doubt in his voice.

He came out of the darkness, and rubbed against his

captor. Almost peevishly Colbie pushed him away. Instantly he was contrite. The situation was too serious for a petty display of anger.

"Sorry," he said. "I'm a little on edge. Come on back."

"I'm subject to the whims of a universal law—gravitation," Deverel said cheerfully. "I'll be along presently. In the meantime, scion of law and order, that cop's mind of yours should be able to figure out what we'll do in the time remaining."

Colbie did not answer, and Deverel went on talking, in his lighthearted way.

"We could eat, and sleep, think a while, and try that reaction business. Or else we wait until our oxygen tanks run low, and then cut a hole in the fabric of our suits. This atmosphere is most likely lethal."

Colbie's mind agilely grabbed a thought from his words. "Wait a minute!" he snapped. "Deverel—maybe I've hit it. We'll sleep!"

He cut the darkness with his beam, throwing it on Deverel's face.

"What do you know about Vulcan?" he demanded.

"What do I know about it?" Deverel cocked his head in curiosity, and then said, "Vulcan was first discovered in the middle of the nineteenth century by a Frenchman who saw a spot moving across the face of the Sun. But nobody thought it was a planet; they thought it was a Sun spot. Later, everybody forgot about it. Then it was discovered to exist in actuality, when the first space flight was made in the twenty-third century.

"It is eight hundred and ninety miles in diameter, presents one face to the Sun, has an extremely eccentric orbit, has a year of three Earth months; its orbit cuts the plane of the ecliptic at a greater angle than Mercury's; it has a high albedo—"

Colbie cut him off. "That's enough. I'm interested in the eccentric orbit. How far is it from the Sun when the planet's nearest, in perihelion, that is?"

"Little under five million."

"In aphelion?"

"Thirty-eight million miles."

Colbie nodded, and again pushed Deverel from him. While the danger both faced had placed their personal relationships in the background, Colbie didn't want to take a chance. At any moment since Deverel had been taken prisoner, Colbie reflected, the outlaw had had an opportunity to turn the tables.

"Vulcan's almost exactly in aphelion now. Listen to this: Suppose we were to take somnolene, and sleep until perihelion, or, rather, near perihelion. The Sun would be—"

Deverel's blue eyes fairly snapped, and his finely cut features lighted up in an expression of revelation. "I've got it!" he exclaimed.

"Certainly. But it doesn't call for that much enthusiasm, does it?" Colbie regarded Deverel curiously. "Are you thinking of the same thing I am?" he demanded.

Deverel hesitated for an instant. He smiled. "I am! You're thinking of the Sun pulling us from—"

"Right. And it seems reasonable, doesn't it? Near perihelion the attraction will be sufficiently powerful to exert a kind of tidal drag on us. We'd be pulled from center of gravity to the inner surface of the day side.

"That would leave us in the same predicaments you mentioned a while ago, except—there'd be no danger of falling back. And, of course," he added with a touch of unleashed irritation, "it'd be like climbing a precipice to reach the hole. But we have to take our chances. No use hanging here, using up oxygen with each idle moment."

Deverel looked at him with an enigmatic expression, and nodded briefly. For a moment Colbie met his eyes with a frown of puzzled doubt; then they bumped against each other again. Colbie said: "You've got somnolene?"

"Got it, but never had occasion to use it."

"It's safe. Carter used it in 2490 when his ship broke down on Uranus. By the time he had it repaired, the fueling station on Ganymede, one of the Moons of Jupiter, was so far away he couldn't make it. He took somnolene, slept fifteen years to conjunction with Jupiter, and made it back from Ganymede none the worse. But we won't have to stay under more than a month—Vulcan makes the rounds in three. How does it sound?"

"Fine. But you needn't ask my advice, since I'm your prisoner, you know."

Colbie's eyes narrowed. He could hardly miss the undercurrent of mockery in the outlaw's manner. But since there was nothing tangible he could put his finger on, he cast the doubt from his mind, at least temporarily.

"Then it's us for somnolene. I don't really place much faith in the idea, but it's a chance, and we couldn't live to perihelion on the oxygen we've got. I wish we could put the stars where they ought to be, as the saying goes, but that's life."

They drifted together again. Colbie smiled a little and, grasping Deverel's shoulders, whirled him around.

"Very sorry," he apologized. "But if you woke up before I did, you might play tricks. There's a look in your eye, my fine fellow. Hands behind."

Deverel's answer to this was to break free, with a sudden twist of his body. He floated away, Colbie's beam calmly playing on him. The outlaw's lips were twisted, almost stubbornly.

Colbie smiled into his eyes. "Oh, no you don't. It's

handcuffs for you, Deverel, or else this." He drew his projector, and leveled it at the outlaw.

For a moment their eyes locked. Deverel tossed his head. "You win," he said gruffly.

After a time he drifted back, and Colbie snapped the cuffs on with a click.

Colbie turned the outlaw around, flashed his beam on the waist of his suit. Beside the belt holding projector holster, and projectile compartments, there was a row of white buttons.

"Somnolene is third on left," muttered Deverel.

Colbie pressed the third on the left. Instantly a thin rod arose, bearing in its grappling hook clutches a pellet of somnolene. Deverel reached out a tongue, and captured the drug. He swallowed it. The rod dropped back into the spacious interior of the suit, folded up inside the mechanism of which it was a part with a click.

"Water," murmured Deverel. "First on right."

Colbie elevated a thin metal tube. Deverel sucked and sighed.

"That'll keep us under a month. Right?"

Jack Colbie grunted. He watched the other man, noted the glazing eyes, the face set in a sleepy half smile.

Then he quickly swallowed his own pellet. He snapped off his beam, and lightlessness in the fullest sense of the word descended. He hung motionless. Deverel suddenly rubbed against him.

"Happy dreams."

"Good night," Colbie responded. He laughed to himself. There'd be no dreams with this sleep, for metabolism in the body ceased entirely with the introduction of somnolene into it.

His thoughts suddenly skipped into haze, and then, for

one second, his mind worked at a furious rate. He found himself saying, "It won't work! It won't work!"

Then he found himself unable to follow the thought. He felt a weight on his eyes, and the darkness of Vulcan's interior rushed in upon his mind. His consciousness dwindled to tiny points of thought. Vulcan—a bubble—not a chance—Kepler! He slept.

He awoke, with the sensation of spinning up from an abyss. Little thoughts came back, added to themselves and presently chained themselves together to perform that miracle called memory. Then he was fully conscious, and conscious of a burst of sound that filled the darkness, and then died away.

"Deverel!" He shouted it. "What the—"

"Oh, you're awake. It's time."

Colbie collected his wits. He drew his flashlight. The beam caught Deverel in the face.

"How long've you been awake?" he demanded. "And what in blue hell was that sound?"

Deverel grinned. "That," he said "was me. I've been awake about two hours. I'm heavier than you, and the somnolene didn't last as long." He expelled a long breath.

"That sound was just one of the devices I've been using to amuse myself. First, when I awoke, I pushed against you to see how far away I could get. It wasn't far. I always drifted back. I became horribly bored, and started shouting like a fiend. I was just wondering if the sound wouldn't be taken up by the cup-shaped sides of Vulcan, and reflected back a thousand times magnified. I haven't got an echo yet, but I'm hoping for one any minute now.

"Then I sang—terrible. You've noticed how flat our

voices are, and that's how, only worse, my song sounded. On Earth there are hundreds of blending echoes for a single sound. There's nothing here for sound to reflect from. And then I gave that last shout you just heard."

"I'm glad I wasn't awake for the singing," Colbie remarked dryly.

He paused, and said slowly, "Bad news, Deverel. Just before I slept, I had a thought. The Sun can't pull us from center."

Deverel evinced no surprise. "I know it," he said calmly. "I've been thinking deeper into the subject than I did before, and have come to the same conclusion. Do you know why, though?"

His arms were twisting around behind his back, trying to ease the stiffness.

"Kepler's Second Law," answered Colbie disconsolately, his eyes on Deverel's twisting arms. "Turn around," he said suddenly. "I'll take those damned things off—must be uncomfortable. And it doesn't make any difference now." He unlocked Deverel's wrists, and repeated, "Kepler's Second Law. The radius vector of a planet describes equal areas in equal times, which is another way of saying that the nearer a planet gets to its primary, the greater is its angular velocity. Which means that centrifugal force equals centrepital."

Deverel nodded. "So we'd have just as much tendency to be thrown toward the night side as to be drawn toward the day side."

They lapsed into a silence which Deverel broke by absently humming an air. Colbie looked at him in surprise.

Deverel shrugged his shoulders. "If we escape, I go to prison. The outlook is the same for me, whether we escape or don't. Hm-m-m. We should've heard those echoes by now, if they're coming at all."

Colbie laughed. He wished he could share Deverel's view, but he decided he wasn't that kind. And then he suddenly wondered if Deverel's air of unconcernedness was based on something he knew that Colbie didn't know. Was there actually a means of escape?

His train of thought was broken when Deverel bumped against him again. He shoved the outlaw away, and then he felt himself spinning, head over heels. Suddenly he swept through the short distance separating him from Deverel, and contacted with a thud. He started spinning again, once, twice, and finally grabbed at Deverel's legs.

"I, too, am gyrating," Deverel murmured, laughter in his subdued tones. He took a quick half spin, and locked his long legs about Colbie's waist.

Colbie put his flashlight in a pocket. "What is it?" he inquired.

"Listen," Deverel replied.

Colbie listened, and heard a murmuring, sighing sound. The murmuring rushed into a whine. Colbie threw his arms around the outlaw. They spun madly, became motionless, and then felt themselves moving at a quickly accelerating speed. Colbie heard a whining, keening sound that gradually grew louder, snapped off, and became a steady, rushing whir.

Then, with an instantaneity that was startling they spun again, gyrating in the opposite direction with such pinwheel rapidity that they lost their holds on each other.

After a moment they crashed together, the metallic parts of their suits clinking dully. Deverel was laughing as he locked his arms about Colbie. Colbie in turn hung on tightly. He had no time to think matters out, save that he knew they were in the grip of a swiftly moving current of gases. They continued to spin, even as they swept forward at constantly increasing speed.

Minutes of furious, driving speed passed. Colbie's mind became fogged, for the swift rotation of his body sent the blood to his head. Dimly, as from a far distance, he could hear a booming, thrashing, at times screaming, sound. He supposed, as in a dream, that numberless gas currents in conflict were causing the bedlam. The cause of the wind he could only dimly suspect.

How long their motion in this direction continued, Colbie did not know. But he calculated it to be some thirty or forty minutes. At the speed they had been going, fully half the distance between center and inner surface must have been consumed. After that time they began decelerating very rapidly. Simultaneously there was a rise in temperature.

Groggily, Colbie hung onto Deverel. To have done otherwise would have subjected them to the bombardment of each other's bodies. Perspiration began leaking through his skin, and soaked his inner clothing. He loosed an arm, and peaked a refrigeration unit up a notch, and gratefully felt the air in his suit cool off. Somewhat irrelevantly he wondered about Deverel's echoes, and decided that if they really had been on the way back to center, they would have been lost by now in shifting volumes of gases.

Gradually they became motionless, both in lateral motion and in rotatory. Somewhere off in the darkness whining, shrieking noises, the product of catapulting winds, still reigned. But here they were for a blessed moment becalmed, swaying back and forth in an indecisive, warm current.

Colbie collected himself, took a deep breath. He released himself from Deverel, and drew his flash. For just a moment he saw the tense, anxious expression on the face of the outlaw, and then it was gone. Deverel was grinning.

"Some wind," he murmured.

"Yes, wind. But why? What caused it?"

Deverel hesitated, and then said, "Well, Colbie, consider. Vulcan's near the Sun, and the Sun's heat worked through the day side crust. The high albedo of the planet's been fighting the heat, but the Sun got so close the heat sank through. The gases on the hot surface became heated, and came in conflict with cooler gases above. Winds would result."

He assumed an expression of alertness; then his eyes rested, for a mocking moment, on Colbie's. Suddenly he threw his arms around Colbie.

"Hang on! Listen!"

Colbie listened. He heard a moaning, dipping cadence that seemed as if it were infinitely distant. It grew in volume. Abruptly it took on a thousand discordant, screaming, weirdly chilling sounds.

Colbie waited apprehensively. Then, as if some imponderable force had hurled itself against them, they felt themselves flung forward, in a straight angle. There was an abrupt sense of acceleration. Whether this was the same direction they had first pursued, or whether it was perpendicular or at an angle to it, Colbie did not know. Again he and Deverel whirled. Again his mental powers were fogged by the onrush of blood to the head.

The wind that bore them shrieked and moaned, and rose to a crescendo roar that culminated in a clap of thunder. Abruptly they were tossed sidewise into the maw of a cooler current, and Colbie supposed they were falling toward the day side. The sudden change of direction did little to help him regain his full faculties.

The current which held them continued its straight course. It bellowed, and crooned, and quivered along false minors that were grotesquely plaintive. Then, point-blank,

24

it met a head wind. It shuddered, broke up into countless tiny currents that spewed off in all directions. The oncoming wind veered off, and the two men found themselves decelerating, hovering in a gentle breeze that cooled them.

Colbie disentangled himself from the outlaw.

"We can't be far from the day side," he remarked, shining his beam on Deverel again.

"We've traveled a good distance," Deverel admitted. "And," he added, "we're going to travel more. Here comes another wind."

Colbie heard it, an awful, hurrying sound. He barely had time to attach himself to Deverel before the wind was on them.

It struck them with the force of a tornado. It plowed into them, took them from the grip of the disinterested current in which they swayed, and gave them a tremendous initial velocity. The shock was too much. They grunted, and lost consciousness.

Colbie regained his senses to find that he still held onto Deverel. They were eddying steadily but slowly. He heard a steady drone, tireless, relentless, and indicative of great speed. Though other sounds could be heard, they were subordinated. There was a tiny, faraway scream; a hissing, insidious whisper; a spasmodic, tearing, angry roar, and all seemed fighting for admittance. And because they could not enter, Colbie felt a sensation of security, as if he were in a sanctuary provided by a swift, kindly current.

He relaxed in relief, though danger had certainly not passed them by. Below somewhere, perhaps only a few miles, was the jagged inner surface of the planet.

He felt Deverel move in his arms. Up to this time the outlaw had been unconscious.

Long moments passed. The outlaw chuckled dervishly in his ear.

"What's amusing?" Colbie shouted above the drone.

"What's amusing?" Deverel reiterated. He laughed again, and stilled himself to say, "Colbie, I'll tell you. But you won't like the joke. I've just been thinking how I'll hate the prison bars, and the workshops on Mercury. I am a desperate criminal who needs freedom, so——"

With a sudden jerk he freed himself. Then he placed his great space boots against Colbie and pushed—hard.

"So," he concluded, "au revoir!" His voice dwindled away into the darkness, and was swept away at the last by the drone.

Though the reason for Deverel's sudden exodus was not apparent, Colbie's reaction was sudden. With one hand he sent a beam of light stabbing into the darkness. With the other, he grabbed for his projector, and found it—gone.

Colbie cursed, and continued to send the beam forth. For one instant he thought he saw Deverel, and with flailing arms he tried to make his way in that direction. He contacted nothing of a solid nature, but still he strove.

At last, swearing steadily, venomously, but in real puzzlement, he relaxed. Then he listened. Nothing but the monotonous drone, and the evanescent, pleading sounds outside, met his ears. Deverel was gone, but where had he intended going?

He abandoned action, and put his mind to work. He was spinning again, but slowly.

Somehow Deverel had known a means of escape from Vulcan's interior. Ever since Colbie had mentioned the Sun, he had known it. Colbie knew that now. And since then his actions had been suspicious. He had been more reluctant than was necessary when Colbie locked his wrists together. He had been restraintive in discussing the currents raging about them. Of course, the convection current was the whole thing.

Colbie cursed at his own idiotic lack of understanding, for now he knew.

The winds! Sun heat had warmed up the day side atmosphere; cooler winds had been pushed and drawn from the central portion of the planet as the day side winds rushed up along the sides of the planet. He and Deverel had been drawn Sunward by falling currents. Erratic currents had grasped at them, some warm, some cooler.

But the main thing was that the gases, in warming, would also expand. Vulcan was filled to capacity with gases produced within itself. The expanding volumes of gas would have to escape. The only avenue of escape was the hole.

Deverel had figured it out, step by step. He knew they would fall toward the day side in the arms of the descending currents. He had kept his secret merely to keep Colbie off guard. It had worked splendidly. Colbie had had both projectors. Deverel had had ample opportunity to confiscate both. Colbie could adequately grasp his motive there.

"Damned good," Colbie muttered angrily, more in resentment against his own stupidity than against Deverel. "First, he'll use reaction to shove himself into the current of escaping gases. That'll leave me out in the cold, unless I'm picked up by the current anyway. Second, if I do escape, I won't be able to push myself toward the surface of Vulcan when I get out. That'll give him plenty of time to effect a good escape, and throw me off his trail. Smart."

He waited patiently. He craned his ears for sound of a shot, but he didn't hear it. Possibly Deverel had not thought reaction necessary; possibly the bedlam of noise swallowed the sound. Colbie didn't know.

The steady drone went on endlessly. Then, when Colbie was beginning to fear that he was merely traveling in a huge circle, the drone changed from its monotone to a struggling, beating roar, like that of surf breaking on rocks. It would die away in a furious churning, surge up again into a poisonous, screaming fury, and then recede again to the sound of rushing waters.

Then its velocity broke, slackened, and its mighty, unchallenged superiority was gone, as currents from a dozen angles smote it. A maelstrom of conflicting winds tore at Colbie. He was caught up in a devil whirl, flung violently about, like a puppet attached to innumerable contrarily pulled strings.

Then another purposeful wind stream caught him, transferred to him a sensation of security, and moved him along at acceleration. The temperature arose swiftly, and Colbie felt a leap of joy. He was in the grip of the escaping current!

A drop of perspiration grew on his nose. He blew it off with a breath expelled upward. He waited, bracing himself for the next shock. It came a soul-wrenching jerk, a burst of speed that eclipsed all others. At the same time the screaming and ranting of the winds opposing each other rose to unprecedented heights, and almost destroyed coherent reasoning in an awful cacophonic blast.

Then it was gone, and all that could be heard was a rising, keening note that eventually passed beyond the limit of audition. Another single sound was born, and rose to nonexistence. And Colbie heard a gurgling, choking, belching, sucking polyphony like the death rattle of a giant. He began spinning, slowly, evenly. He knew now that he was on the way through the crust of Vulcan.

Apprehensively he waited, hoping he would not be brushed against the sides of the hole. But the current was twisting, the region of low pressure at center. The greater pressure on the outside of the column, he reflected, would keep him at the center. A tornado, or twister, did the same thing when it sucked objects up.

A second later, he burst into the cold of Vulcan's night. The stars stared down frigidly, as he was spewed forth.

Eagerly, he looked about. But Deverel was not to be seen, either above or below. He arose swiftly, in the arms of the ascending current. He scanned the billowing, uniformly white surface of the planet from one horizon to the other, but he saw no sign of Deverel. Down below, not more than five or six miles from the outlet, were the two ships, black cruisers anchored from chance, external forces by metal bits that ate deep into the surface.

Deverel was still inside the planet, undoubtedly. Probably he had tried reaction, but the force had sent him the wrong way. It was hardly possible, Colbie reflected, that Deverel would not be thrown out, considering his own ease of escape.

He went up and up. He suddenly saw the Sun, large as Jupiter from Ganymede. Its boiling rays brought beads of perspiration. He kept his refrigeration unit working at full power.

Vulcan receded, its horizons drawing in toward each other. Colbie kept his eyes on the hole. And then—Deverel was erupted!

He came up, tumbling head over heels. He arose at tremendous velocity, a thousand and more feet below Colbie. Colbie watched, saw him draw a projector, and fire it, straight up. Colbie winced as the projectile whizzed past his ear at two miles per second.

Deverel, however, was not attempting to annihilate Colbie. His purpose had been to check his own velocity. He succeeded. He came to a halt. For a moment he was still; then he fired again. The reactionary force sent him spinning awkwardly from the up-blast, and down toward the white, wavy surface of Vulcan.

Colbie was still rising when Deverel landed. In a single leap the outlaw reached his ship. Then he stood in front of it, and waved his arms, both of them. Colbie halfheartedly waved back.

Deverel turned back to the ship, worked on the door for a moment, opened, and stepped into the air lock. The door shut after him.

A few moments elapsed, and then the cruiser rose. With a back firing of rockets, it swiftly disappeared into black, star-speckled space. Colbie kept it in sight as long as he could.

He smiled in chagrin. Skid-rayed! He felt like a child who has missed lessons in school. But he found that he didn't really care. Deverel would escape, yes, but not for long.

Hours later, he started drifting back. Bubble it was, but Vulcan had enough pull to save him from the Sun.

JUPITER TRAP

(*Astounding Stories,* August 1937)

John W. Campbell, Jr., next year to become editor of
Astounding, was writing his series of articles about
the planets at this time. Few writers in years to come
would fail to mention Jupiter's methane and ammonia atmosphere and its fifteen-thousand pounds-
to-the-square-inch atmospheric pressure and its two-
and-a-half-times Earth gravity at the surface. These
surmises were fascinating, and they offered me a
science basis for an interesting scientific situation
which would pose a problem of escape. Follow Colbie as he relentlessly blasts through space along the
friendly-enemy type outlaw Deverel's trail. It is obvious that Deverel will escape, not only because he
understands the laws of physics, but so there can be
another story in the series, *The Men and the Mirror,*
coming up.

Deverel had had seven hours' start on Colbie; it had
taken the officer of the law that long to float down to
Vulcan's surface after the action of expanding gases within
the tiny planet's interior had vomited him miles above it.
In those few hours Deverel had had the opportunity to
vanish into any direction; yet Colbie, using a canny process of elimination, tracked the outlaw to Ganymede.

Not, however, that it did him any good. Colbie was a
good man to have in the interplanetary police force, a
smart man; but he lacked the ability to let his imagination
run rampant. Deverel was different; behind his smiling,
cynical eyes was a mind that worked with the swiftness of

lightning, a mind that never admitted defeat. Or perhaps it was simply that the forces of nature allied themselves with him, gave him hints of secrets that Colbie was denied —as in the Jupiter trap, for instance.

Colbie didn't *know* that Deverel was on Ganymede; he merely suspected it, and fervently hoped that it was so. He knew that all the minor planets—Mercury, Venus, Earth, Mars—were all on the other side of the Sun at that time, and to plot a successful course around the Sun takes a great deal of time and mental energy, the first of which the outlaw had none to spare, the second of which he would not have had the patience to make use of.

He also knew that Jupiter, and its family of worlds, lay in conjunction with Vulcan, that Deverel was running dangerously short in rocket fuel, that it was much less costly to travel in a straight line by first building up velocity and then coasting the rest of the way to Jupiter, where, at Jupiter City, he could refill his tanks.

So Colbie set his course for Jupiter. But, since he, too, was short on fuel, he also had to coast.

It took him ten days to cross that frightful gap between large and small planet, and when he did get in its vicinity, he was tired from the constant watch for meteors. He discovered that Ganymede, Jupiter's second-largest moon—diameter, thirty-two hundred miles—was less than ten thousand miles away; so he made up his mind to land there. Later, he decided Deverel would have experienced the same fatigue, and would have landed also.

Having come to this satisfying conclusion, he had to use further logic in determining at what point Deverel would have landed, but there was a comparatively simple solution to this problem. Years before there had been a fueling station on Ganymede, established to accommodate the great liners that had to make the long trips from the minor planets out to Pluto. But that was before man had learned how to combat the crushing atmospheric pressures and gravitations of such planets as Jupiter, Saturn, Uranus, and Neptune, by the invention of the Jupiter suit. The fueling station—relocated now at Jupiter City—had been abandoned, for the raw materials of rocket fuel were to be found in inexhaustible quantities on Jupiter.

But the buildings were still standing, since the weather effects on Ganymede are practically nonexistent, and any Earthman would have been drawn to their vicinity as if by the action of a magnet.

The unmanned station was located on the floor of a small valley that received more sunlight on the average than any other spot on Ganymede. When it had been built, that had been taken into consideration. Ganymede always presents one face to Jupiter, in its week-long orbit around the planet.

Colbie went to the valley, skimming the rocky, tumbled surface of the planet so that Deverel would have little opportunity to glimpse him from afar. Literally, he stuck his nose over the lip of a precipice that fell sheer to the floor of the valley some hundreds of feet below. The valley was not wide, but it was fairly long. The Sun was the size of a dime, and the mountains threw short, dim, conflicting shadows.

What Colbie saw far exceeded his expectations. Exultantly, he spiraled the ship back up, then zoomed down into the valley. Meteorlike, he cut as near to the edge of the precipice as he could. He turned the ship's nose down, and the ground came up, like a big white hand, to slap him. He jammed on the fore rockets, and grunted under the sudden deceleration produced. The ship came down lightly, settled to rest behind one of the large limestone boulders that lay in profusion across the floor of the valley.

He hurriedly locked his controls. He put on a spacesuit. Probably he could have stood the outside temperature, or even the thin air, but a spacesuit provided for both in a comfortably generous manner.

He swung open the port hatch, leaped out onto the ground, which was composed of a near-white, frozen, vegetationless clay. He stood looking about him. All was silent, motionless—as silent and motionless as only a lifeless planet can be.

Colbie stuck his head around the curve of the limestone boulder. About three hundred odd feet away lay a long, black cruiser. Less than a hundred feet from the cruiser was the shine of an icy lake, worn smooth by thin, timid breezes. On the opposite shore of the frozen lake were three buildings, all in various stages of disrepair, but, in the main, intact. The buildings were not high, but they were long. They had been used to store thousands and thousands of gallons of rocket fuel.

Colbie had been right when he supposed that those structures, so reminiscent of Earth and its peoples, would draw Deverel to their vicinity.

He remained hidden behind the aged, dirty-white boulder. He smiled to himself. Somberly, he swore to himself, that *this* time Deverel would go back with him.

He waited for Deverel to put in an appearance. His patience was his stanchest quality. He became a part of the landscape itself, though he imagined he was well enough hidden from the outlaw, since almost certainly he was leisurely inspecting the crumbling interiors of those lonely, deserted edifices across from the lake.

Colbie waited less than an hour. Then he stiffened, came to his feet. He saw Deverel, and, though four hundred feet of distance shortened the figure of the man, Colbie was sure it was he. He drew his projector, made sure it was charged, and waited.

Deverel came from the building, sauntered slowly toward the lake. He stopped on the shore of the lake, reached out a foot to test its strength, though that must have been a habit of Earthly experience, since for ages the lake must have been frozen solid to its bed. Then he was out on it, walking across slowly.

The outlaw set foot on the barren soil of the lake's shore, and Colbie jumped out from behind his hiding place, and, without parley, pulled the trigger of his weapon. Less than ten feet from where Deverel strode along, a geyser of powdered soil and rock spurted violently into the air.

Colbie shouted at the top of his voice, "Stay where you are, Deverel."

But, ever quick to respond to the stimulus of danger, Deverel did not stay where he was. Near him was a small limestone boulder. He threw himself behind it. Colbie fired again, just missing the outlaw.

There was a moment of tense silence. Then Deverel began to fire back, a steady blast of explosive projectiles that was not intended to annihilate Colbie, but merely to demolish the limestone mass behind which he was hidden.

Colbie had dived behind his shelter again, scared by the vicious fire. But he made ready to adopt Deverel's own tactics. And there he had Deverel at a definite disadvantage.

Calmly, he began to whittle the smaller limestone boulder down, beginning at the top, and progressing more slowly as he came to thicker portions. The thin air became a receptacle to volumes of sound. Powdered rock rained about Colbie. Sometimes larger particles fell on him; but he was not hurt, for gravitation here was slight.

He won sooner than he expected to. He had almost demolished Deverel's protection entirely, when a projectile caused it to split down the middle. The two halves fell away from each other, rolled a short distance, and then settled to rest. Deverel, flat on the ground, lay exposed. For a few seconds, he halfheartedly continued his fire, and Colbie, grinning, allowed him to do so.

Finally, Deverel stood up, shouting out loud, blending both chagrin and admission of defeat into his tones. He threw his weapon in the policeman's direction, and then held up his hands in token of surrender.

Colbie ran across the space separating him from the other, grinning his triumph.

"Hello, Colbie," he said uncordially.

Colbie returned the greeting, and stood looking at the larger man with an exultation which, out of politeness, he tried to conceal.

"Don't look so smug," Deverel snapped, and added in exasperation, "How did you find me?"

Colbie told him. Deverel nodded, a grudging respect in his blue eyes. "That was good work, damned good work. Going to take me back to Earth and jail, aren't you?"

"I was thinking seriously of that."

Deverel scowled. "All right. Let's get started. But I'll tell you this: I don't think I'll go back. I don't know why, either. But I place a lot of faith in miracles."

"It will be a miracle that lets you escape me this time," Colbie promised grimly.

Once within Colbie's ship, the outlaw was placed in irons. Colbie was taking no chances. He put Deverel in the control cabin, right where he could be seen.

Then he applied the power. The ship grated on the

frozen soil of the planet, then swooped upward at a steep angle, swooped upward until the moon drew its horizons together, until Jupiter, monstrous and dangerous, loomed into view, its multicolored face changing both form and variety of color.

Colbie happily piled on acceleration, followed a temporary trajectory to Earth until he could get busy and plot a precise one. But his satisfaction at the agreeable turn of events left little room for the maximum of caution he would have had otherwise.

Deverel sat motionless in his irons, resigned to his fate, within certain limits. He was watching Jupiter, and his thoughts were grim. He didn't want to go back to the hell holes on Mercury that they called jail. But at present, he couldn't see any way out. If only something would happen, one of those miracles he had so hopefully alluded to—

Almost as if his thoughts were conscious prelude to the event, before their minds could grasp the reality of it, the ship was turning head over heels in space. Jupiter was flashing dizzily first through one plate and another, with the whole heavens whizzing around after it as if they were deliberately chasing it. Colbie was thrown backward against the air-defining machinery. Abruptly, there was a sharp hiss as a tender glass tube broke under the impact. He bounced across to the opposite wall, then plunged toward the nose of the ship to collide, destructively, against the instrument panel.

Deverel was sitting tight in his irons, watching with wide eyes as the lights went out. On the instrument board a few bulbs were still burning, and the vision plates were still in operation. Deverel watched the jigsaw of motion. A massive encyclopedia, that had somehow found its way from the living quarters aft, came along. It hit Deverel on the side of the head. Other loose articles began to bombard him, but he was helpless to fend them off.

There was an eerie sense of downward motion, now; the outlaw supposed that it was downward in respect to Jupiter. He watched the mad hodge-podge with the wonder of a child. Colbie, desperately trying to secure a handhold, continued to jerk from one side of the ship to another. Almost battered out of his senses, he accidentally hooked his fingers around the starboard guide rail, and he hung on grimly, clearing his head.

He worked his way around to the instrument panel, and, with what few control levers he had not damaged in his mad flight about the ship, he tried to get the ship on an even keel. There was no response. He tried again. But it was useless. Swearing beneath his breath, he realized that one of those rare accidents had befallen him: although the ship had been traveling at a good clip, a meteor had caught up with it from behind and smashed itself into the stern jets, leaving them fused and useless.

He stood as still as he could, thinking seriously, and heard Deverel murmur with humor, "You were taking me back to Earth. Go on with the story from there."

"Don't be a fool," Colbie snapped coldly. "Do you think this is your miracle?"

"Maybe it is," Deverel said casually. "We're falling toward Jupiter."

"That doesn't mean anything! Not a thing—except that when we land we'll be lost, so lost that it'll be child's play finding that needle they used to talk about!"

Frantically, he worked at his controls again. Definitely, the jets were fused beyond repair. More than that, the lights wouldn't go on; nor were the air rectifiers working. Colbie found himself unable to right the ship by any means, and there is a sickening sensation in the feel of a ship that is not using an axis formed by stem and stern to twirl on.

Finally, Colbie got out the Jupiter suits.

" 'Men—three cheers for the Jupiter suits,' " sang Deverel, taking the line from a popular ballad. He hummed through the bars of the tune and then ended, "They say you can't die in a Jupiter suit. That's almost the truth," he added, and quoted again, " 'You can't get cold and you can't get hot, and the alloy won't crack, no matter what!' "

"It's lucky I have them," Colbie remarked. "Just before I left Earth, the force finally got permission to equip its ships with a couple of the suits each. They're pretty costly; people are allowed to use them only on the big planets, where they have powerful gravities and thousands of pounds atmospheric pressure. They say the alloy they make them out of resembles neutronium, which is about the heaviest substance known, and the hardest. That's why they're so costly, and why they're distributed around so sparingly."

He took Deverel from the irons, pointed to a Jupiter suit. They clambered into the bulky affairs.

The ship was still spinning in that sickening way. Colbie felt sick. Deverel was smiling weakly. "Let's get out," he suggested, as they buckled down their helmets.

Colbie's head was reeling. He was trying to think clearly. He went to an aft compartment, got a pair of handcuffs. He came up behind Deverel, snapped one cuff around his wrist, and the other about his own.

Colbie opened the hatch. There was a gust of air that rushed out into vacuous space and dissipated itself in an expansion that might eventually have touched infinity. Colbie pushed the outlaw after the air, and perforce followed immediately after.

The ship was long and black beside them. To other sides was the starry sky, a sky which, from the interior of a hermetically sealed ship is bewilderingly grand and awesome, even to the initiated, but from without is domineering and frightening. There is no bottom to space. It is an awful sensation to fall—

They were falling, and the ship was falling with them. It was still spinning, though, and dangerously. The two men placed their space boots against the ship, succeeded in shoving themselves from its immediate vicinity. Twenty or thirty feet away, however, it continued to fall with them, true to the axiom that all bodies, no matter what their shapes, sizes, or weights, will fall at equal velocities, providing there is no atmosphere to affect them otherwise.

They felt no sense of weight; their very motion, being the effect of Jupiter's gravitation, was its cancellation. There was nothing but the tiniest sense of acceleration.

Below was the great, poisonously colored disk of Jupiter. In fascination, they watched its gradual growth.

Deverel broke the silence by murmuring, "Jupiter, hard, mean planet—I wonder how he'll treat us. We're liable to land anywhere, Colbie, anywhere on its billions of square miles. Jupiter City might be conceivably less than a hundred miles away, or more conceivably, a hundred thousand. In either case, we wouldn't have the food, air, or luck to get more than fifty miles. That planet is pockmarked with all sorts of mountain ranges, valleys, gorges, and every kind of un-Earthly river and sea. There are big lakes of acids, liquid ammonia, liquid oxygen, and Lord knows what other stuff. It isn't a pretty prospect."

Later, many, many hours later, Deverel suddenly gestured. "There's the great red spot, Colbie—just on the rim. That's good, mighty good. It means we may fall somewhere near Jupiter City, if we watch our weights."

Colbie saw his line of reasoning. The spot, shooting up over the western rim of the planet, would, since Jupiter rotated on its axis in ten hours, disappear over the eastern rim in about five hours. Three hours later, Jupiter City, located on the equator, where gravitation and atmospheric pressure were considerably less than elsewhere, would then be working up over the western rim. Two and a half hours would bring it beneath their present position in space. That gave them ten and a half hours to land.

They could do it, if they regulated their weights. Jupiter suits were necessarily equipped with gravity controls. Of course, out here in space, any variation in their weights meant nothing so far as their downward velocity was concerned, but the moment they struck the atmosphere, it *would* mean something. By decreasing their weight they would decrease inertia, and thus increase the ability of the atmosphere to resist their passage through it. They would fall more slowly, and, if they were careful, they *might* land somewhere near Jupiter City.

The spot, still an enigma in the minds of all men, sloped down the curve of the planet, and disappeared, leaving the breath of a red glow after it. The glow disappeared.

Acceleration had been increasing rapidly. They were so near the planet that it almost blotted out a whole quarter of the sky.

Thirty-eight hours after deserting the ship they felt a new force being evoked about them, and the stars above had suddenly gone almost imperceptibly dimmer; it meant that they had entered the vast atmospheric envelope of the planet.

The stars were taking on distorted appearances; here, where the atmosphere was thin, they even twinkled a little, strongly reminiscent of a little green world which Colbie

41

was beginning to feel he would never see again. Deverel seemed above such sentiments, or at least did not reveal their existence.

He seemed fascinated more than anything else. "I've been on Jupiter only once," he confided. "It was before I began pirating canal boats on Mars. Jupiter's a nasty planet, all right, but it's always interested me. Maybe because it's like me. It's so big, and so unconcerned with the rest of the system. It rolls along out here, takes its leisure going round the Sun—twelve years—and drags nine planets along with it, whether they want to go or not. It's a big chemical workshop. All sorts of marvelous things take place on its surface. It has such a high atmospheric pressure and gravitation that it seems it could do anything it wanted to in any element. When you think about it, it makes you glad you've got on a Jupiter suit."

They could talk without use of radio, now. The atmosphere was thick about them and carried the sounds. The stars were going out and it was becoming utterly dark. There is no sunlight on Jupiter's surface, for the gas blanket completely absorbs or else reflects what little light the Sun can send that far.

They began to decrease their gravity potential. They still had a little over three hours to fall, and at their present rate of speed they would strike the surface of the planet much too soon to leave them within walking distance of Jupiter City.

They watched their chronometers closely, and, because of that fact, time seemed to plod.

They estimated their height above the planet as being only a few miles now, and they experienced sensations of crawling fear. They were falling into darkness, onto the surface of a planet five and a half billion square miles in area. They had estimated the time of their falling as well as they could, however, and, if they had overlooked nothing, Jupiter City *should* be somewhere near, within a five-hundred-mile radius; though, of course, five hundred miles was as bad as a million, so far as traversing it was concerned.

They lived in a world of small, enigmatic noises now. All sorts of noises were rushing up at them from below, above the whir occasioned by friction of their suits with the atmosphere. What were they? Animal life? Avalanches? Or rushing steams? Probably the latter, thought Colbie, or perhaps there was an ocean of some hellish liquid chemical down there, waiting to engulf them. He shuddered.

There were moments of tense waiting. Their nerves were keyed up for the first contact with the surface. It was exhausting. They didn't converse. They only stared down through blackness, vainly trying to find out how far they had to fall. Colbie could have introduced some light into their situation, had he gathered enough presence of mind to remember the search beam built into the breast of his Jupiter suit; but he didn't remember it, nor did Deverel; otherwise they would have saved themselves a good deal of the horror of uncertainty.

Colbie felt a constriction of fright. Something had brushed against his boots.

They touched again. Something had reached out from the darkness with light fingers, or so it seemed. Deverel let out his breath in a loud sigh. They tried to remain in a vertical position so that they might retain a sense of equilibrium should they strike some horizontal surface. But they couldn't. Slowly, they fell sidewise, frantically reaching out with hands that touched nothing.

Again they brushed a surface, and this time began to roll in crazy, slow motion down a steep slope. Abruptly, they came to rest on a hard surface. They lay there, motionless, after that ordeal in which nerves had suffered considerably more than anything else. And they became aware of a constant, forceful bombardment of little missiles that struck them from above.

Simultaneously, they jumped to their feet in that pitch-blackness.

"What was that?" chattered Colbie, as the bombardment continued. Deverel was silent and then laughed. He reminded Colbie of the search beams built into their suits, and snapped his on. Colbie sheepishly slid aside his breast panel and did likewise. Twin shafts of light leaped out, partially piercing masses of swirling white gases.

The little missiles turned out to be nothing more than swiftly falling drops of a white liquid.

"Rain?" exclaimed Colbie, in brief astonishment.

"Must be liquid ammonia," corrected Deverel. "Jupiter doesn't bother with April showers, you know. No, it's so cold there couldn't be any liquid water. It's all ice, and there's probably little of that. They have to make their own water at Jupiter City. But this must be liquid ammonia; this 'rain' is colorless, looks like water, in fact."

Colbie flashed his beam about. He got a blurred impression of swirling white gases, of constantly falling rain. Close inspection showed that the stuff they trod on was worn almost frictionlessly smooth by the eternal fall of liquid ammonia. It had a gradual slope to it, and they followed this slope up until they came to a satin-smooth wall.

Colbie played the beam about, and found it to be a thick spire of basalt that rose up for a short distance, then leveled off. It was this they had first struck. They walked around the column, found it almost perfectly symmetrical. At its foot the rock sloped down at a uniform angle. They started walking down the slope. They came to what looked like a pool of water. Colbie assumed that it was liquid ammonia.

He flashed his beam across this obstruction and brought into stark view a vertical black wall, down which streams of liquid ammonia were running in hasty rivulets. It was about forty feet across the ruffled surface of liquid ammonia to the wall.

Colbie discovered that the wall rose upward indefinitely, for his beam revealed no single break in it. Nor was there a single break in the escarpment to either side. It rose vertically, unflawed by the merest suggestion of a handhold.

They followed the curve of the land, constantly examining the escarpment. After walking for fifteen minutes, they discovered this fact: that, although the escarpment receded at times, drew nearer at times, there was no slightest deviation from its absolutely vertical aspect.

Colbie stopped suddenly, thinking. Then he started walking back up the slope of the land, Deverel perforce following. A minute's walk brought them to the spire they had first examined, and Colbie gave vent to an exasperated curse.

He smiled sourly at Deverel. "Do you see it?"

"See what?"

"That we're on an island! An island in a lake of liquid ammonia; and the lake bounded by the most damnably vertical walls I ever saw." He grunted disgustedly. They fell silent. The rain fell constantly, forcefully, while they stood there, baffled and angry. But one could hardly remain angry at circumstances which anger could not affect.

Deverel was still secured to Colbie by handcuffs. Now he simply twisted his hand slightly; there was a brittle, cracking sound. Colbie whirled like a tiger, his projector out, a snarl contorting his features.

"No alarm, Lieutenant." Deverel smiled. "Why should we tie each other down, since we're in such a bad fix. The cuffs would have snapped anyway. That alloy snaps easily in cold like this—not like the Jupiter suits."

Colbie remained poised in angry uncertainty for a few seconds, and then relaxed, viciously shoving his projector back into its holster.

"What do we do now?" asked the outlaw.

Colbie smiled cynically. "We stand here a while. Then we sit down. Then we get up again. Then, like everybody else slated for death, we'll manage to scrape up some false hope, and we'll take another look around. Then we'll sit down again."

"Interesting," Deverel commented quietly. "I suppose that goes on *ad infinitum*. I don't like the routine, myself. Well, let's sit down anyway."

They sat down.

There was a long silence.

There were gently fitful winds of ammonia gas. Sometimes they could hear the lapping of ammonia against the escarpment. The ammonia rain continued; its fall produced a constant, distantly drumming sound in their ears. But, all in all, these sounds just emphasized the eternal changelessness of the place.

Colbie had the feeling that if he sat there much longer he'd become just as unchanging. His nerves were at the snapping point. Snarling to himself at his impotence, he sprang to his feet, ran to the lake's edge. He followed the shore, flashing his beam in all directions. Deverel watched him disappear into the mists.

He sat motionless, a phantom smile on his face. Whenever he thought deeply, he always wore that phantom smile. He was arriving at various conclusions which might or might not mean something.

When Colbie came back, he said, "Sit down, Lieutenant. Your search has been fruitless."

Colbie sat down.

Deverel lay back on the smooth stuff of the island, sighing. "You know, Colbie, it's entirely possible that we're near the settlement."

"I suppose so," answered Colbie indifferently.

"It's nice to think of the place, isn't it? Especially since it seems as if we'll never see it.

"It's fitted up pretty comfortably. There's Earth food, running water, heated rooms, shows, dancing places, and newspapers—old newspapers. It certainly seems a dream to have that domed city so near and yet so far.

"It's mighty unfriendly outside the dome. Gas everywhere. You can hardly dignify it by the name atmosphere. Red, green, yellow—poisonous stuff—cyanide, ammonia, sulphur. Near the city are mountains, which rise to heights of four and five miles, like knives, and then drop down almost vertical on the other side. Man doesn't know much about them. But he's got the territory around Jupiter City pretty well mapped out, for a radius of thirty or forty miles.

"There are lots of interesting things in that area—geysers and lakes and things like that; all full of a variety of chemicals in a liquid state. There's the Fountain—men call it that—it's a falls of liquid ammonia that spouts right out of the face of a cliff. They can't imagine its source. According to all logic—they measure the force of the falling liquid and can tell the height it falls from—it should originate about five miles up.

"Some explorers went up that high once, and with special instruments they followed the Fountain in its course through the mountain. Five miles up—which is about the highest a mountain ever gets on Jupiter, due to the gravity—they lost track of it. And they didn't find the source. They found that, due to conditions of atmospheric pressure and heat up there, ammonia gas would not condense to liquid. So how could there possibly be a source for the Fountain up that high? Well, it's still a mystery. And there are those funny hills to the south of Jupiter City, Colbie, that are made of the hardest——"

He paused. "Not boring you?"

"Go ahead and talk," invited Colbie. "But it's queer to hear you sentimentalizing about the comforts of home."

But Deverel lay still, saying nothing more. Apparently he had said all he wanted to.

After a while, Colbie stretched out beside him. He felt apathetic. He was not bothered so much about their fate, now that he was quite certain what it was to be. For a while they would live and then they would die. There seemed no other course to follow. Dimly, in his moment of sleepiness, he remembered that time within Vulcan when he had allowed this outlaw beside him all the latitude he wished, because he had been so sure their cause was hopeless. And Deverel had escaped him. But, of course, *this* was different. There really was no way out this time. So he slept—for he was tired. And when he awoke, Deverel was gone.

He searched the island, throwing light into every spot of darkness wherein the outlaw might have secreted himself. He managed to scale the spire that rose unflawed almost in the center of the island; but it was a gesture that indicated his absolute bewilderment.

His bewilderment gave place to a blazing anger directed against himself. Once more Deverel had utilized his remarkable energies of the mind and had escaped the law; once more Colbie had played the fool.

But cursing his own stupidity was no way to solve the questions paramount in his mind.

Where had Deverel gone? What flight of logic had told him there was a place to go to?

Colbie sat down and tried to think it out.

There were these facts to go on: He was on an island about seventy feet in diameter, just about in the center of a lake at least two hundred feet in diameter. The lake was girded by unscaleable walls.

It rained continuously; ammonia rain, it was, that fell without stopping, that came down in torrents, and with considerable force—an eternal downpour. Did that mean anything? Was there any clue there? Thus his thoughts ran, and suddenly something clicked. Did it mean anything? Certainly it did! Why didn't the lake rise? Why didn't it come up and overrun the island? There wasn't any visible outlet; therefore there must be an invisible one!

He stiffened in exultation. That was how Deverel had gained egress from this trap! But, he thought more soberly, if that outlet were subterranean, as it must be, then it would almost positively lead to a point miles below the surface of Jupiter! Why, that was worse than the present predicament!

Deverel must have been crazy, he thought. No, he thought again, Deverel was *not* crazy; he was cunning, and he was the kind of a man who would take a chance when the odds were against him. What then, was the chance which Colbie was overlooking?

He couldn't solve the problem.

He began to think about that singularly queer soliloquy the outlaw had indulged in, and the more he thought about if the more he was convinced that the outlaw had said it with a purpose—perhaps to give Colbie a hint as to where he had gone.

He had laid particular emphasis upon a Jovian phenomenon called, by man, the Fountain. Was it possible that this lake was the Fountain's source? Irritably, he decided it couldn't be. Men of science had proved that the Fountain originated five miles up in the mountains, and that the condensation of liquid ammonia would not take place that high.

So Colbie had to reject the Fountain—almost. He stubbornly believed that Deverel had alluded to the Fountain with a possible solution in mind.

So Colbie arose from his reclining position, walked down to the lake's edge, where he stood looking at the water-clear liquid. He hesitated for but a moment, then walked into the lake.

Its bed sloped down swiftly; Colbie reasoned it must be pretty deep. He walked forward with a steady, unfaltering pace. It came up to his knees, to his hips, to his shoulders. It was then he hesitated again, shivering in chill apprehension. It was the idea of going down into the depths of the unknown that made him almost sick with fear. But he kept on walking, and when the constant bombardment of rain ceased, he knew that his head was beneath the surface.

He took another step forward. His foot touched nothing. He strove to regain his balance, but he fell downward slowly. He could not stay himself. But his fears were unfounded, for he landed on a solid surface, and struggled to his feet. Frantically, he switched on the search beam built into the breast of his suit, though he had wished to conserve his power for later emergencies. The swiftly dimming path of light did little, however, to relieve that abysmal fear of the unknown.

He came to the wall of the lake, noted that it continued in unabated austerity of contour down to the lake's floor. He followed it, one hand scraping it to help him keep his balance.

The lake was quiet, but there was a slight current. Knowledge of where this current must lead made his nerves crawl, but at least there was the comforting assurance that where he went, there was Deverel. Much good it was going to do him.

The current was becoming stronger. He felt as if the flat of a giant hand were urgently pushing him along. He tried to hold back, then, in panic, realized that he couldn't.

So he abandoned himself to the push of the current. He cooled down abruptly. There was no use fighting the unpreventable.

Then he was swept off balance. He began to spin. The liquid about him began to boil violently. He was swept to the right, breathtakingly, and it seemed as if he could hear the liquid humming past him, so swift became his passage. With what little latitude of thought his dizzy brain gave him, he reasoned that he was now in the outlet, a tunnel through the escarpment, probably.

For a few seconds his course was straight. He did not have the optimism to believe it would continue in that manner. Of course, it was bound to make a downward turn. He knew that well enough, and waited for it, waited for that sickening drop down into the bowels of the planet.

But, seemingly, the rigid laws of logic and physics were not adhered to on the crazy planet Jupiter, for the current did not turn down. It turned *up*.

Dumbfounded, Colbie found himself too dazed to hunt for the solution. He didn't think there was a solution. Why, that stream simply *couldn't* turn up!

But it had.

After a while he found himself unable to think clearly anyway. In the long hour of that vertiginous ascent, he was battered repeatedly against the walls of the passage, and though the Jupiter suit, true to its legendary invulnerability, was not affected, Colbie felt the shocks in every bone and muscle in his body.

Turning over and over, on a cock-eyed merry-go-round, he found himself unable to correlate his thought processes with the things that were happening to him. He had not the least idea where he was going, but he wished with all his heart that he would get there.

Abruptly, he was no longer ascending. He was coasting along on a straight course. Somewhere below lay the lake —miles below, it must be. Incredible little lake it was, sending its surplus content into an outlet which went upward, defying the very law of gravitation!

He had risen at a thirty-degree angle, and now he began to drop at even a greater angle, and thus a little faster. Then a great light dawned in him, and he thought he had grasped the truth. But it slipped away from him, even as consciousness slipped away.

He had been losing consciousness gradually. The merciless batterings against the sides of passage were beginning to tell. The last thing he remembered was placing his gravity control at about Earth normal. He was falling, falling fast, and he didn't want to hit too hard. Then the darkness of the tunnel seeped into his mind. He was quite unaware of the remainder of the descent and——

Abruptly, he was conscious of two things: first, a steady, throbbing, rushing, roaring sound that stole into his body and seemed to dominate its pulse beat; second, a strong light that was directed squarely onto his face. He tried to look beyond the beam, but couldn't. Anyway, he knew who it was.

"Feeling better?" Deverel asked, and, when Colbie made an attempt to get to his feet, added, "Stay where you are for a while."

He had a projector in his hand—the deadly hand weapon

of the twenty-third century. He had spoken slowly. Gloom was all around them. The beam itself had to pierce swirling, chaotically colored vapors.

"I knew you'd come along," said the outlaw.

"Did you?"

"Yes. I knew you'd figure it out far enough to enable you to follow me. Of course, I was only acting on guesswork myself. I was not sure I'd turn up safe."

"We're safe?"

"As can be. That's the Fountain you hear—all that rushing and roaring. Falls about a hundred feet from the face of the cliff behind you into a deep lake. I fished you out of the lake. You were floating. You had sense enough to decrease your gravity potential, probably for the same reason I did.

"Now you wonder why I went away without taking you. As I said before, I knew you'd follow. I dropped those hints about the Fountain for that purpose. If I had taken you with me, Colbie, I knew the confusion of it all would give you the chance to get the upper hand again. As it is, you see, I've got the upper hand. I took your projector," he added with humor.

Colbie groaned dismally to himself. Until now he hadn't realized it was gone. "Now what?" he inquired bitterly.

"I want your credentials."

"What?"

"They'll give me immunity in Jupiter City, Colbie. I can get a ship from the garrison. I can escape some place—never mind where, busybody. Give me your credentials."

"If you can get them," snarled Colbie, thrusting out his jaw angrily.

"If you don't give them to me, I'll kill you and take them."

Colbie opened one of the pocket drawers of the Jupiter suit and drew out a long metal tube. He gave it to Deverel, then eyed him questioningly.

"I'm going to Jupiter City," answered the outlaw. "You can follow me—after a while. I sort of like you, Lieutenant, and I couldn't shoot you down in cold blood. By the way, I suppose you've solved the enigma of the Fountain?"

Colbie nodded his head in affirmation.

Deverel said, "Not so mysterious now, is it? Simple, in fact. I thought of the possibility when I went beneath the lake; but I was only acting on guesswork.

"It's possible, Colbie, that you had forgotten the enormous atmospheric pressure on Jupiter, a pressure which would have thwarted man's settlement of the planet had it not been for the discovery of the alloy from which Jupiter suits are made. That pressure is in the order of thousands and thousands of pounds to the square inch; it could raise a liquid to the height of five miles. If you had thought of that pressure, possibly you would also have considered the possibility of a siphon.

"You know the prime requisite of a siphon—that the liquid to be drained away must lie above the point to which it is drained. Well, the source of the Fountain, the lake where we thought we were hopelessly trapped, lies above the mouth of its outlet, the Fountain."

Deverel was talking slowly, in a monotone, perhaps merely to hear his own voice in this solitude of murmuring gases that whirlpooled ceaselessly around.

"Take the ordinary siphoning tube—liquid is rising in the short arm, descending in the long. It is atmospheric pressure and gravitation that makes it possible. Take the ascending part of the hose—the liquid in it weighs less than the liquid in the descending part. All right, the liquid in the descending part falls—gravitation. It has a tendency to produce a vacuum in the hose—right where the siphon turns down at the top. Nature, as you have doubtless heard, abhors a vacuum. Air always tries to fill this vacuum; but in this case it can't get in. Naturally, the air tranmits its pressure—atmospheric pressure—to the liquid, and the liquid goes up, preventing such a catastrophic occurrence as a vacuum.

"In this case, the liquid was ammonia; the siphoning tube was a tunnel through the mountains; and the outlet was the so-called Fountain. There you have all the requisites for a siphon—perfect."

Colbie had listened patiently; he knew well enough the principle of the siphon. He grinned wryly to himself. He had known the principle of the siphon so well that he remembered only that water, under atmospheric pressure, will rise thirty-three feet; but that had been on Earth, and never for a moment had he considered that Jupiter's immense atmospheric pressure was capable of raising a liquid of the order of density of water to a height a thousand times and more as great. Deverel, of course, had considered it!

But Colbie was able to pick the obvious flaw, or apparent flaw. "But," he pointed out, "the tunnel had to be filled before siphoning operations could start; otherwise there would be no tendency to a vacuum."

Deverel was thoughtfully silent for a moment. "That's a good point, but I don't think man will ever know the answer. All he can do is theorize. Theorizing, I'd say that once upon a time, a long time ago, the lake was far up in mountain region, and the tunnel was just a plain everyday subterranean outlet, ending at the Fountain.

"Then the whole mountain range buckled under the stress of weight distribution; the lake dropped; the tunnel was bent into the form of a siphoning tube. It wasn't choked up, so the liquid—it might have been, up that high, some other liquid gas than ammonia—kept on flowing." He nodded in satisfaction. "That's probably the answer, at that."

He was silent. Murky gases danced fantastically through the beam of light.

Colbie lay on the strangely spongy soil, held there by the threat of the outlaw's weapon. He said, "We're using up oxygen."

Deverel snapped, "How long can you breathe on what you've got?"

"Thirty-six hours," answered Colbie, after inspecting the gauge.

Deverel growled to himself, "It's foolish things like this that are going to put me behind bars! Well, you can get to Jupiter City in about twelve hours. But I want you to stay here the other twenty-four."

Colbie's eyes widened in surprise. He started to say something and stopped. "I see," he said, looking at the leveled weapon. He met Deverel's eyes and said solemnly, "You have my word of honor that I won't move any nearer Jupiter City than I am at present for twenty-four hours."

Deverel dropped the beam from Colbie's face and turned it on his own. He smiled in a friendly fashion. "All right, Lieutenant," he said softly. "You're a good fellow—I hope the feeling is mutual. Well, good-bye! I'll try to keep out of your way hereafter—for both our sakes I wish you would do the same!"

He turned quickly in the direction of Jupiter City. The search beam built into the breast of his Jupiter suit turned with him, and almost immediately, save for the faint glow of reflection from the thick gases that raced across the surface of the planet, he was lost to sight.

Colbie lay back on the ground, because his body was still an inferno of aches and pains. Bitterly, he began his twenty-four-hour wait; bitterly, because he resented his helplessness. Deverel wouldn't have much trouble getting a ship, and then there'd be the whole solar system that Colbie would have to go over as with a comb.

He reflected that Deverel's escape was not his fault so much as he had believed. Natural phenomena had a way of helping Deverel and forgetting him entirely.

THE MEN AND THE MIRROR
(*Astounding Science-Fiction,* July 1938)

If the known planets are not properly endowed to fit the scientific problem, one must tailor a planet to the measurements. In science fiction this is easy and often necessary. The planet Cyclops was new to the solar system on the long night I wrote the entire 15,000 words of the third Colbie-Deverel story. It fulfilled all conditions for the working out of the ideal science problem I had in mind. A "minor" error unfortunately did creep in; minor?—and surprising to me the author. When you come to the latter part of the novelette where the two men escape their trap, try to realize that the men actually (according to Robert D. Swisher's mathematical proof which appeared in a later issue) were spinning on their own axes at about 500,000 r.p.m.!

Mr. Swisher's letter follows the story.

The men were plunging down the gently curving surface of the mirror.

Above them were the stars of the universe, whose light was caught by the mirror, radiated and reradiated by its concave surface, and, unimpaired, was flung back into space as a conglomerate glow.

There were two of these men. One was Edward Deverel, a worldly wise, carefree giant of a man whose profession —up until the recent past—had been that of pirating canal boats on the planet Mars. The other, a hard, powerful man, was Lieutenant John Colbie, whose assignment it was to apprehend this corsair of the canals.

Theirs was a real predicament, for they were unable to produce, at present, any means of escape from the prison this smooth, shining, deep bowl of a mirror presented.

As to how it all came about——

When Colbie, after his twelve-hour trek along the ammonia river which ran from the lake into which the Fountain poured its noxious ammonia liquids, finally reached Jupiter City, he was in a state of fatigue under which his muscles, every one of them, seemed to scream out a protest. He pressed the buzzer that let those within the airlock understand that he was demanding admittance, and was decidedly relieved to see the huge valve swing open, throwing a glow of luminescence on the wildly swirling gases that raced across the surface of that mighty, poisonous planet Jupiter. Two men came forward. They covered him with hand weapons, and urged him inside the lock. The keeper of the lock desired to know Colbie's business, and Colbie demanded that he be taken before the commander of the garrison—who was also mayor of the city—as things had, of necessity, to be run on a military basis.

Riding through the streets of the city, he was both thrilled and awed, after that tortuous ordeal in the wilds of Jupiter, by the consciousness of the great genius of the human race—that it was able, in the face of so many killing difficulties, to erect this domed city, so well equipped with the luxuries of Earthly life. For outside the city there was a pressure of fifteen thousand pounds to the square inch. There was a gravitation two and a half times that of Earth. There was not a breatheable drop of oxygen in the atmosphere, and not a ray of light ever penetrated the vast cloud layer to the planet's surface. But man had built the city, and it would remain forever, so solidly and efficiently was it constructed.

When Colbie came before the dome commander, that individual listened to his story, eyeing him keenly in the meanwhile.

"So you're Lieutenant John Colbie, of the Interplanetary Police Force," he mused. "Yet, not less than thirty-six hours ago, another man stood before me and presented proof that he was John Colbie. One of you is wrong, I'd say, and no mistake about it."

"I've told you my story—that other man was a criminal, Edward Deverel by name, and I was put on his trail. I caught up with him on Vulcan, near the Sun, and we found it was hollow by the simple expedient of falling through a cavity on its surface. I had Deverel prisoner then, but he proved a bit too smart for me. We were trapped there, well enough, at the center of gravity. But he figured that the gases filling the planet's interior would expand as the planet came to perihelion, thus forming currents which Deverel used to his advantage in escaping the trap and eluding me at the same time. I found him again, but we were wrecked above Jupiter, fell into a pit with a liquid ammonia lake at the bottom. And Deverel, using, I'll have to admit, remarkably astute powers of deduction, figured that the lake drained by means of a siphon of some height. He eluded me that way, and I was left in the pit. I finally caught on—from some deliberate hints he had let drop—and followed him through the siphon. But he was waiting for me at the other end, demanded my credentials, and extracted from me a promise that I'd stay where I was for twenty-four hours." Colbie grinned in slight mirth. "So after twenty-four hours I came on. And now he's gone."

" 'Fraid he is," admitted the other. "I had no reason to suspect he was an impostor, so I gave him a ship. Come to think of it, he seemed in a mighty hurry. Hm-m-m. How can I identify you as Lieutenant John Colbie?"

"Easy," snapped Colbie. "I'm not unknown. There must be a few IPF men in the city. Let some of them identify me."

"Good idea." The man grimaced. "Something I should have done with the other man. However, that's past. No use replotting an orbit you've swung. I'll hunt up an IPF man or two."

And this he did. Within the space of a few hours, the commander had no doubt that the man who stood before him was one Lieutenant John Colbie, a native of Earth, and in the service of the Interplanetary Police Force.

"Well, we'll outfit you again, Lieutenant," he assured Colbie. "What's your course of action after that?"

Colbie, lolling in a deep chair, bathed, resplendent in borrowed clothing and refreshingly combed hair, cigarette drooping from a corner of his square lips, said, "My assignment was to apprehend a certain criminal; those are my orders. I just have to keep on trying."

"Not if things go as they have," said the other, smiling in such a manner that his sarcasm should have been without edge; but he saw immediately that he had said the wrong thing, for Colbie's eyes narrowed half angrily. "Sorry, he added quickly. And then apologetically, "Don't blame you a bit. Must be a sore point. How come you aren't in any especial hurry?" He deftly changed the subject.

"I should say I'm not in a hurry!" Colbie exclaimed feelingly. "I've been space-tied for a few months now, and I have to stuff a few of the civilized benefits into my life now and then. There's no need for haste, anyway. Only way I can find Deverel is by deducing his destination, then going there."

"Where do you think he went?" queried the other man interestedly.

"The new planet. I notice there's quite a lot about it in the papers. It's been making its way into the solar system for the past five or six months, I understand. It's a real wanderer—probably been zipping through interstellar space for ages. There's a good chance that's where Deverel's gone. He's curious, insanely curious about all things bizarre, and he won't be able to resist it—I hope," he added.

"Good lead, anyway. It'll be a worthwhile experience, too. No exploring parties have set foot on it. You two— if Deverel is there—will be the first to set foot on it. Hope you have good luck, this time," he added sincerely.

Colbie drew smoke into lungs that had not known cigarette smoke for a full half-year. "If there's any doubt in your mind, commander, let me assure you that Deverel's already up for trial, as far as my capturing him is concerned. Yes, I feel it in my bones. He's going back with me, this time."

The two men then looked up statistics on the new planet. It was a large sphere of celestial flotsam, somewhere near five thousand miles in diameter, of extremely low density for its bulk. It was traveling at the good clip of eighty-two miles per second toward the Sun, but it was estimated that the speed would be cut in half by a near passage by Jupiter. Finally it would take up an orbit that would be located somewhere between those of Jupiter and Neptune.

Shooting through space at furious velocity in his new cruiser, Colbie's lips were set and grim. His nerves were on edge. There was a flame in his brain. Truth to tell, he was so furious at Deverel's repeated escapes that the more he thought about it, the less he found himself able to think straight.

He could see the new plant as a small, gray dot against the ubiquitous veil of stars. It was not yet named, but was destined to be called Cyclops, for a reason to be seen. And with the passing hours it grew in apparent size, until, seven days after Colbie had shot upward into space, fighting Jupiter's gravitational fingers, it was a vast bulk in the heavens less than ten thousand miles distant. Colbie dived for it. He still had enormous speed, and was checking it with the greatest deceleration he could stand. When he came near enough to the planet, he used its gravitation as a further check. He started to circle it—and forthwith saw the "eye" of Cyclops staring up at him.

It was a mirror—a concave reflector, rather. But it looked like the eye of the planet, an eye that reflected starlight. Starlight, yes, because it was a reflector that caught the rays of the stars and threw them back to space. Indeed, Colbie, gazing on it awestruck, could see no slightest difference between the brilliance of the stars and the brilliance of that colossal mirror.

"Lord!" he whispered to himself, feeling half-reverent. He suddenly had a sensation of smallness, and realized in that second what an infinitesimal part of the universe he was. He lived for only the fraction of a second and surely was no larger than a sub-electron. For that mirror was artificial, had been fabricated by the powerful tools and intelligence of a race which had certainly lived at least thousands, perhaps millions of years ago. Who could tell how far Cyclops had traveled, plunging at steady pace across the void that separates our solar system from the nearest star? Who could tell the manner of people who had constructed it? One could only say that they had been engineers on a scale which human beings could not at present comprehend.

The mirror was perfect. Colbie took various readings on it, after the first mighty upsurge of awe had ebbed away. He found the diameter, about two miles less than a thousand; the depth, an approximate three hundred; and the shape, perfectly circular, perfectly curved. The albedo was so close to *1* that his instruments could not measure the infinitesimal fraction that it lacked!

And thereat, Colbie sat down and whistled loud and long. Man knew of no perfect reflector; it was deemed impossible, in fact. All materials will reflect light in some small degree, but more often the greater amount is absorbed. But the material of this colossus among reflectors reflected all light save an absolutely negligible amount of that which impinged on its surface. For Colbie knew that *some* of it was certainly absorbed—he did not believe in impossibilities. It was impossible that that mirror didn't absorb some light. His instruments had been unable to measure it, but of course there were instruments on Earth that would measure that absorption when the time came for it. But they would have to be delicate indeed. Even at that, however, the albedo of this mirror was a thing almost beyond belief, and certainly beyond comprehension.

The mirror disappeared around the curve of the planet as Colbie's ship plunged on, decreasing its velocity slowly but surely. Colbie forced his thoughts once more to the issue paramount in his mind—that of locating Deverel. But his exciting discovery of the mirror stayed in the back of his mind, and he was determined to know more abut it. And he did; more thoroughly, in fact, than he liked at the time.

He now had his velocity under control. Hoping that Deverel had not detected his presence above the new planet, he gave himself up to the one problem that was perplexing him—where would Deverel have landed? Near the mirror; that was a certainty. Somewhere near the rim of the giant reflector—but that was anywhere on a circle three and a half thousand miles in circumference.

He finally resolved to scour the area in which Deverel would have landed. Training his single telescope downward so that it would sweep the entire area, he applied his photo-amplifiers to the light received, and then, keeping at a distance of about fifty miles from the surface of the planet so that Deverel could not possibly sight him with the naked eye, he darted around that circle at low speed, eye glued to the eyepiece of the telescope. He hoped thus to see the outlaw's ship.

And he did. It lay at the base of one of those mountains of Cyclops that flaunted a sharp peak thousands of feet up into the sky. That mountain swept down to foothills that terminated abruptly in a level plain scarcely more than seven or eight miles from the rim of the great mirror.

Colbie sighed in lusty relief, entirely glad that his assumption of Deverel's destination had now been proven absolutely correct.

Shooting the ship upward, and then, keeping that single landmark—the mountain—in view, he came up behind it, and, by dint of much use of forward, stern, and under jets, jockeyed the cruiser to rest far enough around the curve of the mountain so that the outlaw should not note his advent.

He put out a vial to draw in a sample of the planet's

atmosphere, but as he had with good reason suspected, that atmosphere was nonexitsent. The undistorted brightness of the stars had almost made him sure of it. He struggled into a spacesuit, buckled on his weapons, attached oxygen tank, screwed down his helmet, opened the air-lock and jumped down to the planet's surface. It was hard. Examining it, he found that it consisted of ores in a frozen, earthy state. Whether this was true of the entire planet he did not know.

He started around the curved base of the mountain, and, after the first mile, discovered that traveling across the surface of Cyclops was a terrific task. The planet was seamed and cracked in dozens of places; great gaping cracks which presented definite handicaps to a safe journey of any length. He found that he had to take precautions indeed, and often searched extensively for crevices narrow enough to leap with safety. He worried along, taking his time, but he was beginning to realize that he might not have as much of that at his disposal as he had indicated to the dome commander back on Jupiter.

So that, after a good many hours, he rounded the breast of the mountain and caught the black shine of Deverel's falsely acquired ship.

But he saw nothing of Deverel.

He threw himself to the ground. Suddenly he was painfully conscious that his heart was thumping. The thought of physical danger in no way caused this condition—he was simply afraid that Deverel might elude capture again by putting his tricky mentality to work. The competition between these two—law and disorder personified—had become a personal contest. Truth to tell, the IP man respected and rather admired Deverel's uncanny ability to escape him, not the fact that he had escaped. Colbie had to bring him back, but respected Deverel's unusual genius at escaping tight spots. But—he had to bring the man in, or admit the outlaw a better man than he.

In this uneasy state of mind, he lay there, projector out. It could shoot explosive missiles at thousands of feet per second, and was, in this, the twenty-third century, the ultimate in destructive hand weapons.

Now, as he lay there, his eyes constantly on the ship and the area about, he turned his thoughts in a new direction. In the name of all that was holy, why had Deverel come here? Hadn't he realized it was the first place Colbie would look? Certainly he must have known it. Then why had he come?

Colbie thought he saw the answer. Deverel had planned on leaving this planet long before the space policeman had arrived. He had had a full thirty-six hours' start on Colbie, and he decided that would give him enough time for the opportunity he so craved—to visit this new planet, and determine to his own satisfaction whether or not there was anything about it which would satisfy that love he had for the bizarre.

He had had sufficient time. Sufficient time to satisfy himself as to the nature of the mirror; sufficient time to leave again, and break up his trail in the trackless wastes of space.

But he hadn't left.

Why?

And then Colbie began to feel acute mental discomfort. And the longer he lay there, the worse it became. He became conscience stricken. And why? Because Deverel might be lying in there sick, and Colbie could not risk coming out into the open until he knew absolutely Deverel's whereabouts. And perhaps Deverel lay in there dying. Space sickness is a recognized malady, and it is not infrequent. It is ascribed to any number of causes, among which are noted positive and negative deceleration, a missing vital element in synthetic air, and the lack of gravitation. Its only cure is absolute rest under a decent gravitation. And—such a cure was impossible for a man who was dependent on no one but himself.

Colbie squirmed uncomfortably. "The fool might be dying!" he snapped angrily to himself. "While I'm lying here. But I can't give myself away."

But his nerves grew more and more tense. He dreaded the thought of Deverel sick in there while he was able to give him help. And in the end he sprang to his feet, determined he wouldn't let the uncertainty of the situation wear on him any longer.

And then his radio receiver woke to life, and screeched calmly though waveringly, "You're out there, Colbie. You *would* be there. Listen—" the voice dwindled away, and then came back in renewed strength. "I'm sick, Colbie, rottenly sick. I think I'm going to do the death act. It's the stomach that really hurts, though there's the ears too. They hurt, too, and they send the blind staggers right through the brain. I'm sweating—" The voice ebbed, rushed back. "If you want to—come in and give me a hand—will you? Then you can take me back—" The voice groaned off, and sliding sounds came through the receiver.

But already Colbie was tearing out into the open, racing across the space separating him from the ship, a wave of pity for the helpless man breaking over him.

The outer valve was open. Colbie climbed in, drew it shut, manipulated the controls of the inner valve, and debouched into the ship proper.

He was now amidships, standing opposite the lazaret.

Forward was the control cabin and vital machinery, abaft, in the stern compartment, were sleeping and living quarters.

Colbie bounded aft, swung through a door, and saw a pitiable sight indeed. The room was incredibly littered with such items as soiled clothing, and dishes with the scum of meals dried onto them. In the middle of the room was a table, and on that table an electric fan was whirling full blast, flinging a steady current of air upon a man who lay stark naked on a bunk which seemed the ultimate in human filth.

Deverel lay there, twisting, squirming, panting, moaning, his eyes rolling, and rivulets of sweat bubbling up from his queerly yellow skin, and flowing down to encounter a plain, stained mattress.

The first thing Colbie did was to snap off that venomous, killing fan. In fact, to sweep it from the table with one blow of his open palm. The next was to take Deverel's pulse. It was quick, dangerously high, but certainly not predicting the close approach of death. In another day it might have ceased altogether, but at present there was plenty of chance.

Deverel's eyes lolled over to Colbie's, and his lips drew back painfully over handsome white teeth.

"Glad you came," he whispered, and then his head dropped back and his eyes closed. He was not asleep; the knowledge that he was now in the hands of a competent person sent him into a dead faint.

Colbie knew what to do in cases like this. He went forward to the control room, manipulated oxygen tank valves, and increased the quantity of oxygen in the air. He got all the clean linen he could find, and bathed Deverel from head to foot in lukewarm water. He turned the mattress over, put on clean sheets, and then lifted Deverel lightly as a baby back onto it. Then he stuck a thermometer into the outlaw's mouth.

He cleaned the room, occupying a full hour in washing dishes with a minimum of valuable water. Then he took meats and vegetables from the refrigerator, where they had doubtless reposed for months perfectly frozen, and started a pot of soup.

And that was all he could do for a while.

He sat down and waited, taking many readings on the thermometer.

And Deverel's temperature went down. His breathing became even, and then he slept. Thirteen hours later he awoke.

"Hi, Lieutenant," he said.

"Hi, yourself!" Colbie put down the magazine with which he had been really enjoying himself for the first time in months. "How's the temperature?" he inquired.

"Gone. Thanks a lot," he added carelessly, but he was serious. "You know I mean it, too."

"Sure." Colbie waved it aside. "A pleasure—I was glad to do it, y' know." He fingered the pages of the magazine abstractedly. He jerked a thumb. "How'd you know I was out there?"

"Didn't *know* it." Deverel laughed. "It's a cinch if you weren't out there you wouldn't have heard me say I knew you were."

"That's right." Colbie laughed, too, and blue eyes and gray eyes met each other in mutual amusement. "Like some soup?"

Deverel said enthusiastically that he did. So that these two men, mutually respecting enemies of each other, sat down and ate for all the world as if each was an affectionate friend of the other.

For many days life was easy. No grueling flights through harsh space. No anxieties. No dread of death to come. No fear of insanely impersonal meteors. Here on Cyclops, the planet of the great mirror, living was a pleasure.

Deverel regained his health. He was finally able to get out of bed and walk around. With that done, it was not long before Deverel was considered a well man once more. Of course, the old life then had to be recognized. There had been a tacit understanding between the two men—for a little while their personal relationships did not stand. That was fair.

But that understanding had to be sundered eventually, and Deverel did not put the time off. The moment he felt his strength had returned in full measure, he said: "Well, it's been fun while it lasted. But it's time for us to sort of assume our natural antagonisms. So you put me in irons—right away. Or I'll give you a swift, underhanded poke to the jaw."

Colbie regarded him judicially. "Fair enough," he conceded. "You wouldn't mind getting me about the heaviest pair of leg and arm irons from the lazaret, would you?" he inquired quizzically.

"Not at all," murmured Deverel politely.

"Wait a minute," Colbie said uneasily. He leaned forward. "Now look. Did you notice the mirror?"

"Certainly. And damned curious about it, too."

"And I. Now suppose we let this unwritten pact of mutual noninterference drag on for a while, just enough to allow us to explore? Y'know, I haven't got a time limit on me—"

"Oh"—Deverel waved a scornful hand—"neither have I. Let's let it drag on, shall we?" he said in the unconscious manner of a youngster excited over the prospect

of a pleasing new toy. "You've got my promise, Colbie—
I won't try to get away."

They saluted each other with a grin, and forthwith
made ready for their adventure in exploration.

Sleep was the first preparation. After a good many hours,
they set off across the gouged, forbidding plain. The stars
looked down at them unwinkingly through the vacuum
separating them from Cyclops' harsh terrain. Behind the
men loomed the sharp, high peaks of the mountain in
whose proximity Deverel had put down his stolen cruiser.

They were decked out as completely as they deemed
advisable. They had oxygen, water, and food for at least
a day. Colbie had decided not to carry his projector. It
was a clumsy weapon, and he saw no possible use for it.
Thus, attached by a two-hundred-foot hank of rope, which
was suited in composition to the demands the cold and
vacuum of space might make upon it, they wended their
starlit way across Cyclops. When they were not using the
rope fording dangerous chasms, they wound it up about
them. They progressed steadily toward the rim of the reflector which probably had been constructed long before
man had made the first full stride toward harmonized
society.

Twice, Colbie slipped at the termination of a leap which
taxed all his physical powers, and twice would have
plunged into the apparently bottomless gorges below; and
twice Deverel braced himself against the rims of the pits,
and pulled the Interplanetary man back to safety. In
both cases they made extended searches for narrower
crevices.

Slowly but surely they worked their way to the rim,
and finally struck level country. The last mile was a true

plain, so unmarred that they suspected it must have been smoothed over artificially at some long-gone period. It struck Colbie that this would have been a much better place for Deverel to have put his ship down. Deverel explained that at the moment the first spasm of sickness had hit him, he was not in a frame of mind to care where he landed.

They came, then, to the rim.

They regarded with awe the black wall. It was composed of some dully hued metal. It stretched away from them in a slow curve that lost itself to their eyes many miles to either side of them. It was perfectly formed and unmarred in the slightest particular, about twice as tall as a man.

Deverel struck a pose, and said vibrantly, "The mirror!" But certainly he was not unshaken by the anciently constructed reflector.

Colbie put in wonderingly, "Some things a man can't believe. I wonder how old this thing is—wonder who made it—how they made it! Lord, what engineers they must have been! What a job!"

"What a contract for the firm that landed the bid!" Deverel put in, smiling. "What do you say we top it? I've got an itch to see it firsthand—touch it."

Colbie nodded, and Deverel braced himself against the wall, forming a cup with his heavily gloved hands. "Up you go! But once you get up," he warned, "careful you don't topple. That'd mean trouble in large doses."

"Don't worry about that," Colbie said grimly. "If any one falls, it's going to be you, not me."

He put one foot in the outlaw's hands. Deverel heaved. Colbie shot up and caught both hands around the rim, which sloped inward. That done, he drew himself upward so that he was sitting carefully on the rim, facing Deverel.

With much effort and care, he drew Deverel beside him, and then, as if with mutual consent, they twisted their heads and sent their eyes out over the great mirror.

At once, all sense of perspective and balance left them. Light from all directions smote them, blinded them, sent a haze into their minds. Downward and to all sides and above, there was light. In fact, the light of the stars and the light of the mirror were indistinguishable in the split second when that bewildering sensation of instability struck them. Colbie thought fleetingly and in panic that he was poised upside down on the most insecure foothold in the universe. He could not decide, in that split second, which was the true sky.

So—he clutched at the wrong sky, and toppled over the rim.

Deverel, feeling precisely the same sensations, would have recovered in time had not the rope attaching him to Colbie forcefully jerked at him a second before he had fully decided which way was up. So they both fell down the angle of the mirror, and were, in a second, shooting haphazardly, horridly, through an interminable pressing mist of light and nothing but light.

They were plunging downward so swiftly, and yet so lightly, that they might have been wafted along on an intangible beam of force. For they felt nothing. Not the slightest sensation of *sliding*—only a sense of acceleration *downward*.

After that first moment of heart-stopping horror, after the first panic, the first moment of unutterable vertigo had passed, Colbie's nerves started quivering violently. Deliberately he quieted them by closing his eyes and clenching his fists. Then he opened fists and eyes both, and looked around for Deverel. Deverel was about five feet behind him.

Deverel was looking at him from eyes that were extremely concerned.

"And I said be careful," he snapped angrily. Colbie started to open his lips with hot words, but Deverel waved a hand disgustedly. "I know, I know. My fault, too." He drew a long breath and occupied himself putting his head where his feet were.

Colbie did the same, and then very gingerly tried to stay his fall, by pressing his hand and feet on the surface of the mirror. This had not the slightest effect on his position or his velocity. He found that it was extremely difficult to twist his body except by flinging his arms around, but he accomplished this not by any aid the mirror gave him. His hands in no slightest degree rubbed against the mirror's surface. In fact, he felt no sensation which told him that his hands might have touched a surface. It was as if he had run a finger over a vat of some viscous slime, as if the slime had imparted no heat, no cold, had not adhered to his finger, had not impeded its motion in any way, had merely guided it along a path determined by its own surface!

He closed his eyes painfully. The trend of his thoughts hinted of insanity. He tried to analyze his sensations. He was falling. Falling straight down, at the acceleration the gravity of this planet gave his body. But he knew he was merely gliding along at a downward angle. He was simply being guided by a substance which in no degree impeded the action of gravity. That must mean—

No friction!

The words exploded in his brain—and exploded crazily from his mouth. *"No friction!"*

Deverel stared at him, and then frantically made tests. He tried to rub that surface. He felt nothing, nothing that held his hand back—as if it had slid along infinitely smooth ice.

"You're right," he said, staring stupidly. "That's what it must be. Hell—it's frictionless!" And then he cried, "But that can't be!" and his lips twitched. "There can't be anything that's frictionless. You know that. It can't be done!"

Colbie shook his head as one speaking to a child. "No, Deverel," he found himself saying in a kindly voice, an insistent but pitying voice, "it has no rub. You put your hand on it and push. And does it hold your hand back? No." He shook his head sadly. "They made this stuff frictionless."

And as they shot downward into the sea of light, they held each other with their dumbfounded eyes.

The outlaw sharply shook his head. "We're making fools of ourselves. Let's face it. There isn't any friction. Now—now we're up against something."

"I know it."

Colbie almost drunkenly squirmed around, and finally maneuvered until he was sitting, his feet crossed under him, his eyes trained hypnotically into the downward distance. Or was there any distance? There was no horizon. The stars, and the conglomerate glow of the mirror that was the absolute reflection of the stars, merged with each other.

"We've got to pull ourselves together," he said stubbornly. "Let's think this out. We've got to get used to it."

"Right." And Deverel did the first sensible thing by twisting and looking behind him. They had toppled over the rim of the mirror almost exactly two minutes ago, and though their velocity had steadily been mounting, there was a horizon back there which could be seen. It was mainly indicated by that lofty, slowly rising mountain which loomed up against the rim of the mirror. He felt that it was a good landmark—somehow, that was the place they had to get back to.

"Now look," he said seriously to Colbie, "let's talk this over." His voice was slightly metallic as it came through Colbie's earphones. "Before I landed on this planet I took some readings on that mirror same as you, and I guess I came to the same conclusions.

"Long ago, maybe a million years, there was a race of men—or beings—who lived on a planet that circled a sun just like ours, perhaps. They had a satellite, this planet we're on. They were engineers on a monster scale. I have no doubt they could have remade their planet, and even their solar system, exactly to suit themselves—and maybe they did. But they made this satellite over to suit themselves, that's certain. They gouged out—how I wouldn't know—a section of this planet that corresponded to the bottom part of a sphere. The radius of that sphere—I figured it—is about 1600 miles out in space. Then, so help me—I wouldn't know this, either—they coated that gouged-out surface with some substance which, when it hardened, formed an absolutely smooth surface. You came to the same conclusions I did, didn't you? That it was such a perfect reflector you couldn't measure the amount it didn't reflect?"

Colbie, listening with interest, nodded. "And we should have seen that such a good reflector would be frictionless, too. Couldn't be any other way. And say!" he exclaimed. "This stuff can't be frictionless. We knew it couldn't reflect *all* light. It simply reflects all but a negligible amount of light, and it's got a negligible amount of friction, too!"

"That's right!" Deverel was genuinely relieved. "That idea of no friction at all had me going cuckoo. 'Course not—there can't be any surface that's got no friction at all. The molecular state of matter forbids it. No matter how close you crowd the molecules, they still make an infinitesimally bumpy surface.

"Now why did they make the mirror? Only reason I can see—power. They must have had a heat engine. It generated power in huge amounts, undoubtedly, and perhaps the power they took in that way was broadcast back to their planet. Or perhaps it was a weapon—another mirror, plane this time, which could rotate and train a searing beam of heat on an enemy ship. Would that ship blister! And they might have been able to rotate this satellite at will, too—

"Then something happened. Those people lost their satellite. Maybe their own planet exploded. Maybe their sun exploded, and this planet went shooting away, and finally our Sun grabbed it.

"And that's a fair explanation—the only one, as far as I see. Unless, of course, it was meant to be something that was in the experimental stage and was never completed."

"The magical mirror," Colbie interspersed softly. But neither of them then knew exactly what magical characteristics it did possess.

For a moment they were silent. "Well"—Deverel had a shrug in his voice—"we can't do anything now—can we? Shall we eat?"

"Why not?"

They ate in the strange manner necessitated by spacesuits. By buttons in a niche outside their suits they manipulated levers which reached into a complicated mechanism, pulling out food pills—tasteless things—and water, which they sucked through a tube.

"Now," said Deverel, smacking his lips as if he had

just eaten a square meal, "this is just another situation, and not a fairy tale. Proved it by eating, which is so mortal it's disgusting. Where we bound?"

"For the bottom—"

"Ho—not at all! We're almost at bottom now—notice how the angle's been straightening out? It's almost 180° now. Let's see. Phew!" He had looked at his chronometer. "We've fallen three hundred miles in something like eight or nine minutes." Colbie started to protest, but the outlaw said, "Sure, to all intents and purposes we've simply fallen three hundred miles—the depth of the mirror. Remember, there isn't any friction that'd hold us back, and the inclined surface we came down on just guided us. And that means we're going to bounce right back to the other rim—see?"

"Ye gods, yes!" yelled Colbie, then grimaced. "But we won't quite reach the rim. Just that damnably small amount of friction will hold us back fifty or some feet. If there weren't any friction things would be simple— we'd reach the other rim exactly."

"Sure. And climb over. Gravity gave us the momentum going down, but she'll occupy herself taking it away at the same rate going up."

While they had been talking, they had passed bottom— quite definitely. They were going up, for the angle was slowly but surely increasing.

"We won't make it," Colbie said disconsolately. "There's the rub."

In the thoughtfully melancholy voice of the Danish prince, Deverel muttered, "Aye, there's the rub; for in that sleep of death, what dreams may come, when we have shuffled off this mortal coil, must give us pause."

"And that's appropriate, isn't it!" Colbie sneered.

"I played Hamlet once. Long time ago, of course, but I was pretty good. You know that second act scene where he—"

"Skip it! Forget it—I don't want to hear it. Let's get on. There is this friction—infinitesimal. It doesn't help at all when you try to change or retard your motion; but in the long run, it'll build up a total resistance great enough to keep us from the rim."

"Check, check, and check," agreed the outlaw, touching the fingers of his left hand with the index finger of his right.

"That's our situation. Looks hopeless."

"Maybe," Deverel declared. "Let me add some further facts. We're dropping down at an acceleration of twelve feet a second per second. At bottom, three hundred miles down, we had a terrific final velocity. Don't know exactly what it is, but there's a formula for it. Going up, gravity will be right on our tails, lopping off twelve feet of speed for every second. Notice I say up and down. I mean it. Our angular speed is something else again, and is certainly much greater."

Then, as he saw Colbie's impatient look, "I don't know how we get out. Normally, when you get in some place, you go out the same way—but they closed the door on us. And, of course, I don't see how we can change direction."

The IP man crossed his legs under him the other way for a change. He squinted upward. "Getting near top again. Damn that light. After a while, I'll go blind."

"Shut your eyes," Deverel told him callously, then, "Lord," he remarked whimsically, his cynical, yet friendly, eyes crinkling. "I'm glad we're what we are, Colbie. You have to chase me and I always feel obliged to run. Then we run into the most interesting experiences. I've had plenty of good times looting canal boats on Mars—did I ever tell you how hard it was squeezing the rings off the Empress' fingers? I used plenty of soap and water—and she was horrified at the way I wasted the water—but somehow I'm glad they got after me. And you are, too," he added as if in self-defense.

"Sure," Colbie remarked. "But in a way I'm not. You're a likeable fellow. I admit it. But you haven't got the instinct to help make an organized unit of society—you're a gear out of mesh. 'Course, there's others like you—but it's you I have to take in. I suppose I'll do it, too."

"Forgetting the mix-up we're in?"

"No. Just trying to match your own superb confidence in crises like this one."

"*Touché.*" The outlaw grinned. "Any ideas to match your confidence?"

"Not a shard."

"Me either—yet. By the way"—and here Deverel regarded Colbie thoughtfully—"I'm keeping anything I learn to myself—anything that might get us out, I mean."

"Meaning?" Colbie's eyes hardened.

"I'll sell what I know for a price."

"Ho! Freedom, I guess!" Colbie said sardonically.

"Well—not that, exactly. I'll tell you what it is, if I ever get anything to sell."

Colbie studied him, shrugged his shoulders carelessly. He looked over his shoulder, but he didn't see the approaching rim.

"Our angle's much steeper." Deverel followed his thought. "The rim isn't far away. Couple minutes yet."

"We won't make it though," Colbie said regretfully, "unless there's something else we don't know anything about."

In a few minutes, they saw the rim outlined against the black sides of an uneven mountain range which might have been set back from the rim anywhere from ten to twenty miles. They regarded its stubborn approach with anxiety.

So slowly it came toward them—and so rapidly their velocity was being decreased to the zero point! Nerves tensed, fists clenched, eyes strained. But intuitively, rather than from any deliberate mental calculation, they felt that they would not reach it. Their velocity was simply not enough.

And it wasn't. Slowly—compared to their earlier enormous velocities—they rose toward the rim which was so painfully near, yet so infinitely difficult to reach. One moment, then, they were rising; the next, falling. There had been no pause, or if there had been it was nestled close to that infinitesimal space of time which man will never measure. They began to fall.

In a voice that held worlds of chagrin—true to human nature, he had not given up hope—Colbie said. "Missed it—by about ten vertical feet, as a close guess. Next time we swing across this damned mirror we'll miss it by twenty feet."

"Something like that," Deverel agreed abstractedly. At the moment they had fallen, he had noted the time down to the exact fraction of a second. And he kept it in mind. Not that he had any idea of its ultimate benefit then, but he felt it might be a good thing to know. "Let's see," he was muttering to himself, and using Colbie's phrase, went on, "the time for one swing across—"

And he didn't finish the sentence. For an idea, a conception so alluring, so utterly startling, leaped into his mind, that he drew his breath inward through his suddenly meeting teeth. "Lord!" he whispered, and almost as if he were stunned, he dropped back, lying full length, his head cupped in the palms of his joined hands. And he saw the stars.

The two men were zooming along at a good fast clip that was building on itself. They were guided by the frictionless stuff of the mirror, and pulled by the force of gravity.

And above were the stars. So cold, so remote, so harshly, quietly beautiful. Deverel was looking at them, hard. They were exciting stars. They never changed their position as a whole. They looked the same as when they—the men— had gone plunging down the curve of the mirror.

While Deverel lay there on his back, his brow wrinkled in thought, Colbie watched him, watched him for a good many minutes, while they plummeted into the depths of the shining bowl. In an incredibly short time, they reached bottom—and Colbie grew tired of trying to read the outlaw's thoughts. He tried to rise to his feet. He went through a number of gyrations, which left him lying facedown, looking at his own reflections.

Deverel had come out of his brown study, and was watching amusedly. "If there were a large enough area on the soles of your feet, m'lad, you could stand easily enough. But when you sit down, the center of gravity of your body is considerably lowered, and it's easy. So you'll never stand up unless by some miracle of balance."

This bit of wisdom was apparent. Colbie sat down, drew the water tube into his mouth, and sucked with abandon. Then he regarded Deverel knowingly. "Been thinking, eh? What about?"

"The mirror," Deverel replied solemnly. "I have to keep it to myself, though—sorry!"

"Likely!" There was a tigerish snarl implied in Colbie's voice overtones.

Deverel's worldly wise eyes grew sardonic. "Sure—I've been doing a lot of figuring, and I've found out a lot of stuff. Interesting, unusual. But there's something missing, Colbie—something I can't put my finger on. If I had it—and I will get it—I could get us out of here. Any suggestions?" he concluded, regarding Colbie sidewise out of a laughing eye.

"If I had them," pointedly, "I'd keep 'em. By the way, are you being fair? Withholding information? I'm referring to your promise—that you wouldn't try to get away."

"I did make a promise, just as you said—that I wouldn't try to get away. And I haven't. And I won't until you tell me it's all right if I try. Get it?" He fixed Colbie with a rigidly extended index finger, and went on in tight tones of significance. "Let's be ourselves from now on, Colbie—outlaw and cop! Right now, we're just partners in adventure. But you, just by saying so, can make us what we really are—and I'd be your prisoner. D'you see? Do that, Colbie, and I'll get us out of here!"

Colbie felt a slow flush rising to his face. Suddenly he felt utterly humiliated; felt as if his intelligence had been insulted and mocked at. Colbie's voice exploded, an eruption of searing wrath. "No! Listen," he went on in a low, deadly, flat voice, "the answer is no. No from now on. I don't give a damn. I don't give a damn if we slide back and forth here for eternity—that's what we'll do if you wait for me to give in to you and your damned insulting demand. You've got the brass—" Colbie choked apoplectically, and stopped. He waved his arms helpessly, glaring at the other man. After a while he went on, his voice now even, "You suggest I haven't got the mentality or the resource to find my—our—may out of here. Maybe I haven't. Maybe I'm a damned dummy. But I'll tell you something that's going to make you squirm; you're going to see *me* out-bluff *you!* And *you*'re going to give in to *me!* Remember it."

He sank back, glaring.

Deverel's eyes were popping. "Well!" he exclaimed in astonishment. "Phew! Glad you got that off your chest— you sure take the fits!"

A lot of thought went on under Deverel's helmet, and in a way they amused him. But they were all directed toward one end—escape. This was a new Colbie, an undreamed-of Colbie, he saw here, and he was going to be a tough nut to crack! So Deverel finally said, "You're going to outbluff me, you said."

"Sure. Now, ever, and always. Something else, my dear mental marvel—it's you that's going to do the thinking." His voice was contemptuous. "Now, go ahead and use that so superior gray matter you're claiming."

Deverel's lips twitched. He said, shrugging, "If that's the way you want it. But you're crazy."

Colbie refused to answer.

"Well." The outlaw laughed lightly. "Now we've got our own personal feud mapped out. We won't be on speaking terms for maybe two or three hours. Incidentally, we'll be bored to death. We won't even enjoy ourselves the least bit. That's the way people do when they're mad at each other. If I were a kid, or if we were medium-close relatives, I'd say all right—but we're two grown men."

"I get it." Colbie put a grin on his face.

"Good!" Deverel exclaimed. "Now where are we, Colbie? Near the top again. There's the rim, too!"

It was true. The rim was there—but it was not the same section of the rim from which they had dropped. Deverel realized it. That mountain, that landmark, did not show up against the rim. They had gone across the mirror twice. By common sense, they should have returned to their starting point. But had they returned, Deverel would have been startled indeed.

They came to the apex of the second trip across—and dropped back, once more missing it by an additional ten vertical feet. Once more they plunged downward into the depths of the shining bowl.

On the way down, Colbie was silent. Unable to help himself, his thoughts began to revolve. How could they get out? But his thoughts revolved futilely. He was unable to look at the matter objectively. Had he been solving a puzzle on paper, the answer would have come soon enough. He was well enough equipped on the laws of motion to have solved it. But, being a part of the brain-teaser himself, he was helpless.

But undoubtedly he should have noticed that the position of the stars in the heavens never changed.

They passed bottom, went sloping upward again, in a monotony of evenly decreasing speed that was maddening, at least to Colbie.

Deverel was not silent. He occupied himself in a frivolous manner, talking, laughing, cracking jokes. He enjoyed himself thoroughly. He could make himself at home anywhere, and in the strangest circumstances. It was one of his admirable qualities.

Finally he called, "How about it, Lieutenant? Making any headway?"

Colbie came out of it. "Know less than I did before," he admitted sadly. The light of the stars, and the light which the mirror so faithfully threw back into space, were beginning to irritate him, too.

"Damn shame." Deverel sounded regretful. "I've got a lot of dope on this strange vale o' paradise," he added sadly, "but I can't find the missing link that'd put it to some advantage. And to be frank, the time to put it to the

best advantage will be in less than an hour. A crucial moment, I mean." He was staring intently at Colbie.

"Damn the crucial moment," Colbie said coldly.

"Well, there'll be several crucial moments," Deverel
said, laughing softly. "The best possible times for us to get
out—but I don't know yet how we'll get out. You say I
have to do the thinking? But it won't hurt if we talk
things over a little, will it?"

Colbie said it was all right with him. After all, the
whole thing was up to Deverel from now on. No number
of solutions would help if Deverel didn't give in.

They discussed the color of the strange substance. Did
it have one? No, certainly not; it absorbed no light, hence
was the color of any light it reflected. Could they, as a
single system of two bodies, change their direction of motion? No. They were a closed system, and as such had a
single center of gravity which would continue on its present
course forever, unless some outside force intervened. They
could jerk, they could squirm, but for every action in one
direction, there would be equal reaction in the other. Was
this substance either hot or cold as determined by human
senses? No. For it could absorb no heat, nor could it,
therefore, transmit heat. The first would convey the impression of coldness, the second that of warmth—

It was an amusing subject, and exhaustless. But Deverel
plucked no fruit from its many branches. They were still
hopelessly marooned within the bowl of the incredible
mirror.

They hit the apex of the third swing across the great
mirror—and fell downward again. They bounced back up
from the bottom, zoomed upward through the sea of
luminescence, fell downward again the fifth time.

And Deverel said, "It's coming. It's here. The first Crucial Moment. But we have to pass it up."

The sixth apex dwindled away, found Deverel looking longingly at the sharply rising mountain which he had placed in his head as a landmark, "the place they had to get back to."

"I know when we have to get out," he told Colbie anxiously, "but the how of it knocks me! Every trip across we take, we fall nearer the bottom by ten feet. Right now we're about sixty feet below the plane of the rim of the mirror. How are we going to rise that sixty feet?"

"You have me there," said Colbie nonchalantly.

Deverel regarded him seriously. Colbie was an uncaring idiot—didn't seem to give a damn whether they got out or not. But Deverel was beginning to feel whole new quantities of respect for the IP man. There was certainly more to him than he had hitherto suspected. He smiled. "Still holding out?"

Colbie said he was.

"Well, you know *I* won't give in." Deverel said harshly, "I'm supposed to be damned fool enough to think my way back to Earth with you, back to jail. I've outbluffed better men than you, Colbie, and I'll stick this one out, too. Are we going to be damned fools? You know, if this was off my mind, I could devote myself a lot better to the one problem that fuddles me up."

But Colbie said that he was sorry he couldn't help the outlaw get the suspense off his mind. And Deverel's teeth closed with a snap. Colbie, looking at the hard sardonic features, wondered vaguely, perhaps with a slight inward shudder, what would be the outcome of it all.

Then ensued utter weariness. For interminable minute after interminable minute, they swept dizzyingly down and up through the pressing, aching mist of light. Their eyes became tortured, their brains became inflamed, their muscles stiffened, their nerves jangled. They became irritable and touchy. The monotony was man-killing, especially in view of the fact that the manner of their salvation was yet a thing of the future—or perhaps a thing of no solution.

Deverel was up against a blank wall, and his every word had a snarl in it. "There's some way it can be done," he insisted, as they were dropping down after the tenth plunge across the great mirror. "And I have to find it 'soon. We're a hundred feet below the rim now. You could help me, Colbie—you've the brains for it, I know you have. But you're lazy, damn it. You insist on sitting back there and letting me do all the thinking. Suggest something, won't you?"

Colbie answered seriously, "Deverel, I have been thinking. But it's no good. What is it you know? What strange characteristics has the mirror got that both you and I don't already know?" He paused, shaking his head. "I can't see the trees for the forest—I'll admit it." He was genuinely sorry he couldn't help, and was more than a little touched by the outlaw's desperate search for the final link in the chain he had evidently fabricated. "Why not tell me what it's all about?" he suggested. "Maybe I can go on from what you've found out."

"No sale!" Deverel snorted angrily. "What I know is my trump card—you'd know as much as I do. Wouldn't do me any good."

"Won't do you any good, anyway—unless you give in." Colbie grinned easily.

"And you can bet everything you've got I won't!" Deverel snapped. And then looked queerly at Colbie. "You really have made up your mind, haven't you?" he demanded. He shrugged his shoulders sulkily. "But maybe you'll change it. That's what I'm banking on, anyway. You're not the type that can hold out forever."

Colbie shrugged his own shoulders in indifference, and then crossed his legs a different way. Thinking better of it, he lay flat on his back, and by virtue of swinging his arms one way and his legs the other, started to whirl about. Elsewhere, the action might have seemed childish, but here it was one of a strictly limited number of amusements.

While this aimless gyration, which, once started, continued unabated, may have amused Colbie at first, it very soon had a much different effect. Abruptly he sat up—still spinning lazily—and stared at Deverel. A slow grin appeared on his lips, went into temporary eclipse as he turned around, and appeared again as the rope holding them together wound up about him. "Your difficulty," he asked judiciously, "lies in being unable to make up for that hundred feet or so we've lost to friction, I take it?"

Deverel looked at him keenly and nodded.

Colbie's face split in a slow, broad grin. "I haven't got it all figured out. I said I'd let you do that. But I know how to make up for that difference. It takes cooperation, and maybe if you know how to do it, you'll give me the rest of that information sooner. Because I won't cooperate till you do. You think what I was doing, and you'll get it."

Deverel looked at him blankly. Then—"I've got it!" he gurgled. "I knew it could be done—and it's easy!"

He was talking rapidly, excitedly. "I've got the whole thing worked out, now. Everything I need! It's only a question of waiting. Two or three more times across the mirror— Now listen," he went on rapidly. "You have to tell me it's all right. This'll get us out, both of us. You will, won't you?" he demanded anxiously.

Then he saw Colbie's mask of a face and shouted furiously, "Don't be a damned fool, Colbie! You don't want to die, do you? You know you won't be able to stand death from lack of water and food—you know it! Now's the time to make up your mind." He was feverish.

"I made up my mind quite a while ago," Colbie pointed out. "If I hadn't, I wouldn't have contributed your clinching link just now."

Deverel laughed harshly. "You're going to stick with it," he jeered. "You're going to let a principle kill you! Well, I'm going to let it kill me, too—and I'm not as scared of death as you are. In fact, it'd be better if I did die; I've got too much hell in store for me, one way and another. So I don't really care. How do you like that?" he ripped out savagely.

"It's all right with me—I always knew you didn't give much of a damn about anything, Deverel." He smiled disarmingly.

Deverel regarded him in blank amazement, an amazement that swiftly turned into sheer, obvious admiration. Until that moment, Deverel had doubted that Colbie was sure of his intentions; now he knew it, and the knowledge gave him a new picture of Colbie.

Colbie yawned; and then Deverel's rage apparently broke all bounds. He called Colbie every foul name under the Sun, reviled him with the unprintable verbal scum of innumerable space ports—and then stopped short.

"Hell, I didn't mean that," he muttered. He waved a hand. "Sorry—I mean it. It's just that"—he summoned a grin—"there went the second Crucial Moment. Rather, the minute we drop down from the eleventh apex—there it goes. It's about a minute away. We're now, to all intents and purposes, a mean one hundred ten feet below the rim. Phew!"

"What are these crucial moments?" Colbie inquired in genuine bewilderment.

Deverel laughed in amused disgust. "There are several of them—I think. And the more of them we pass up, the more crucial the next one is. Get it? At last we come to the Final Crucial Moment! And after we pass that up—" Deverel shook his head. "After that, there's no more hope. No more Crucial Moments." After a while, he said listlessly, "I'll tell you when they come around."

They swept down and they swept up. Angles decreased and angles increased. The rim loomed up through the gloom of light, and dropped away. Constant acceleration, followed by just as constant deceleration. And light and still more light and nothing else but light.

Two men against the magical mirror!

Seventeen times the rim dropped away, and each time they approached it was farther away—ten feet higher than before. And then Deverel remarked wearily, "The third Crucial Moment—one hundred seventy feet below the rim." He cocked an eye—a bleary eye—at Colbie, who was so exhausted and blinded by the incessant play of light from the mirror that he was apathetic. "What are you thinking about?"

"Just waiting," Colbie returned tiredly, "for you to give the word!"

Deverel laughed harshly. "And I'll never give it. Listen. In less than an hour comes the—"

"The fourth Crucial Moment," put in Colbie acidly.

"Wrong. The final." He waited for this to take effect, but it had none at all. Then he snarled, "You're going to hold out—good Lord!" For a moment he was speechless, glaring at the other man. Then unaccountably, he laughed. "We're two of a kind—two stubborn fools. I didn't know you had it in you," he remarked frankly. "I really believe you're going to—" and he broke off.

"That I'm going to hold out past the time that really

means something to us?" Colbie asked him quizzically. He nodded slowly.

Deverel sank back in disgust.

They topped the eighteenth, the nineteenth, the twentieth apex. Deverel was jumpy, irritated. "About half an hour," he said nervously. "That's all we've got. I mean it. When that time goes, then we kiss life good-bye. I wish you'd see reason, Colbie. Either we both die—or I go free, and you live, too, and we're just as if we never came to this planet. Just think of that—life again!"

Deverel watched Colbie intently, but the IP man was absolutely unaffected. The outlaw had been hoping against hope that Colbie would, in the last vital moments, give in. He had determined to wait that long, just on the chance. Now that chance was definitely out, and Deverel had to play a card he had long ago decided to use if worse came to worst. It might win—and it might lose.

So in the next few moments—with the verve and ability of a natural actor (he *had* played Hamlet when he was a younger man)—he increased his nervousness, the desperation of his manner, the snarl in his voice.

"Twenty-five minutes, Colbie. Give us plenty of time." Colbie was obdurate. They were on the twenty-second trip across. Deverel's rasping voice went on later, "Twenty minutes. And here comes the rim."

The rim came toward them, slowly. More and more slowly, and then gently started dropping away. The twenty-third trip.

"Fifteen minutes, Colbie." Deverel's voice had the rasp of a buzz saw in it. He was actually nervous now. The amount of time was pretty small. So that suddenly he said in a tone of voice that was deprived of every trace of moisture, "Colbie."

Colbie met his eyes, and what he saw there made his own open wider.

"You guessed it, Colbie." The outlaw's tone was dull. He spread his hands. "I'm done. I've cracked. Good Lord!" he burst out. "You don't give a damn! That's what gets me—I can't understand it. Listen—you may think I'm scared to die, that I'm not the kind of fellow I've painted myself to be—but I am. I'm careless with my life. I won't care at all when my number's due. What I can't stand is the fact that it isn't due! There's a way out. And it's only your stubborn refusal that's blocking the way. But I guess when you come down to it, it's me—"

"It's I—" Colbie corrected mildly.

"It's I that's blocking the way. So I give up. You win. You're the world-beater of this crowd. You're the champion holder-outer, the prince of don't-give-a-damners! Colbie, you've got me in tears. Honest, I feel like blubbering like a kid. I can't understand you—sitting there—" he groped.

The IP man regarded Deverel steadily. "You're funny," he muttered. "I knew you'd give in, just because of that. You have dash—impulsiveness—a quick love of life. I'm just a stolid space-cop."

And Deverel suddenly thrust out his jaw angrily. "I gave in, didn't I? And don't think I haven't got half a notion to take it back. I'm capable of it." His eyes challenged the other's.

Colbie said slowly, "No. Don't do it—forget it. We were fools—you decided not to be one. That's all there is to it." Once more he met the eyes of the other man, this time thoughtfully, then he nodded his head in slow determination. His head came up, and a sparkle entered his eyes.

"What do we do?" he demanded. "Spill it—let's get out

of this forsaken place. I don't like the lighting arrangements! Come on!"

Deverel went into action.

"Wind yourself up on this rope," his voice cracked out, full of the energy of real desperation now. "Closer—come on! All right." He braced his feet against Colbie, and pushed. Colbie went whirling dizzily away, the rope uncoiling. He came to the end of the rope. Deverel then pulled in such a manner that he utilized to the fullest extent Colbie's rotatory motion. Colbie came spinning back, winding up. Deverel lashed out with his feet. Colbie unwound again, this time in a new direction. Time after time he came back, whirled away again. Deverel manipulated Colbie in the same way a small boy does a certain toy called the jo-jo.

Swiftly, each was swinging around the other in an ellipse with a shifting axis.

"Get it?" panted Deverel. "We've got a circular motion started. It isn't affecting our course in the slightest, though. We're a closed system. For every action a reaction. I'm swinging around you, too. Now, you stop spinning—it isn't necessary now." Colbie flailed about with his arms and, in the course of two revolutions, swung around Deverel in a true circle. And all the while they were hurtling up the slope of the mirror, at a rate dictated by no other force than the retarding power of gravity.

Deverel was gasping. "Now—draw up on the rope. Pulls us nearer the center of the circle we're making and we go faster—our angular velocity increases. Now we're going."

And they were. By dint of prodigious exertions, they worked their angular velocity up to such a point that the centrifugal force was putting a terrific strain on their laboring lungs.

And finally the outlaw gasped, "Enough! We're going plenty fast. If we go any faster, we'll split wide open. We'd keep on whirling like this until the slight bit of friction wore it down—that is, if we didn't use it to escape this trap. And we're going to use it, too! The rim should be along in—two minutes, seventeen seconds flat. Oh, yes, I figured that out to the hair's breadth."

Suddenly he was shouting out loud, "And there it is— the rim! Now, look, honest to God, I don't know which of us is going over." His eyes feverishly watched the approach of the rim, whenever it swung into his line of vision. It was etched against the mountains. Throbbing seconds beat away into the past. Colbie's pulses were hammering. How often afterward he thought of the snapping suspense the looming mirror engendered in him then! It was like a monster—mysterious and brutal. Deverel's voice came again, "I think it's going to be you. It *has* to be you! Yes!

"We're a closed system, remember. Now say we have an explosion. You fly that way, I fly the other. But we each retain the kinetic energy given us by centrifugal force."

Cocking a wild, red-rimmed, bleary eye on the approaching rim, he coiled himself up two feet nearer Colbie. They gyrated more swiftly. Colbie shouted in protest.

Deverel snarled, "Can't help in. The rope has to be parallel to the rim the minute we hit the apex." He blinked his eyes to get the sweat out, looked at the chronometer above his eyes. Seven seconds to go. Deverel was shuddering—he had so damned many things to do at once. He had to regulate their angular velocity—his timing sense— the sense which tells us how many whole steps we can make to reach a curb exactly—was telling him how many gyrations they would make in order to hang poised, for an infinitesimal second, parallel to the rim. With one hand, he had to extract a razor-sharp knife from an outside space kit. And he had to keep an eye on his chronometer, for he had to know exactly when they reached the apex of this, the twenty-third trip across the great mirror.

And perhaps the greatest miracle of that whole insane adventure was that everything worked itself out just as Deverel was planning. The rope, its human weights swinging dizzily at its ends, came parallel to the mirror's rim on the exact, nonexisting moment they reached the climb's apex. And in that exact moment, Deverel slashed at the rope close to where it was fastened about him.

Colbie experienced no change of pace—simply a sudden release of pressure. The operation had been smoothly performed. At the exact moment when they, as a single system, had no upward and no downward motion, Deverel had severed the rope. Colbie simply shot straight forward the rim at the velocity he had been rotating at that particular moment.

He plummeted up the slope of the mirror, gravity now definitely fighting him. He lost twelve feet in upward velocity every second. Would the kinetic energy his body now contained be sufficient to stave off that deadly deceleration? Would gravity whittle it down to zero, somewhere below the rim.

"Colbie," he gritted, speaking softly to himself, "if you've never prayed before, try it now!"

And perhaps the prayers did the trick, or it might have been the computations Deverel's keen brain worked out. Using the factors of their individual weights on this planet, and the two-hundred-foot-length of rope, and the time for one revolution, he had known the approximate kinetic energy each man would develop, had known that Colbie would go over the rim with a liberal margin to spare.

Up past the rim Colbie shot. Over the rim—and up

into space. And there, fifty feet above the planet, he stopped rising. The moment of falling was heart-stopping. His spacesuit was tough—but would it stand the strain? He didn't have much time to theorize about it. He hit, and he hit hard. He felt as if every bone in his body was crushed in the moment before his consciousness faded away.

When he came back to consciousness, he knew a sharp, agonizing pain below the knee of his right leg. "Broken," he thought dismally, and grimaced as he almost involuntarily tried to move the injured member. He couldn't move it at all.

Then the thought of Deverel came back. Good Lord, he was still on the mirror!

"Deverel!" he shouted.

A cheery voice came back. "All here and right as rain." Then the voice became anxious. "What's wrong? I was trying to get in touch with you."

"Broken leg, I guess."

"Hurt?"

"Damnably!" Colbie gritted his teeth.

"I was afraid something like that would happen," the outlaw answered with sympathy. "I'm sorry it had to be you—I would have taken the rap if we'd have swung around right. But we didn't. That was my gamble for escape."

"How are you getting out?" Colbie demanded. Then in sudden panic, "And what if *you* break a leg?"

"Ho! I'll get out, and I won't break a leg either. I have to travel across the mirror, you know, and I'll lose ten vertical feet. How far did you fall?" he asked anxiously. Colbie told him. "Fine! Not bad at all for a rough calc."

"You did a fine job all around," Colbie told him feelingly. "That's right, you'll go over the rim, too. You've got gravitational *and* centrifugal force acting on you."

"Now listen, Colbie, you're on the wrong part of the rim, d'you know that?"

No, Colbie hadn't known it. So their ships were on the other side?

"No, not on the other side. About a sixth of the circle of the rim around from where you are."

"Well, then, where are you bound?"

"For the ships."

Colbie gasped. "You're crazy! You're headed directly opposite from where I am."

"Oh, no, I'm not," Deverel sang sweetly. "I'm headed right for a point on the mirror a sixth of its rim removed from you in the direction the planet rotates. Now quit gasping like a fish, and listen to the most gorgeous and unbelievable part of this whole adventure. Do you think we went straight across the mirror?"

"Certainly!"

"We didn't! Now here's the bombshell—" He paused, and then said, *"We were the bob of a pendulum!"*

"What?" Colbie shouted it in dismay. "Lord, Deverel, you're crazy, crazy as a loon! A pendulum! We weren't hanging from anything, from a string, or cable or—Lord!"

"Getting it?" The voice was sympathetic. "Don't you see? We *were* a pendulum. And the beautiful part was that we didn't need to hang from anything so we could vibrate. A string, or something like that, would have ruined the effect entirely. As it is, we were a perfect, simple pendulum, the which that has, so far, existed only in theory! See, there wasn't any friction, and there was a perfect vacuum. There was just gravity. It pulled us down and up and down and up and down and up. And there was a force which wouldn't let us travel in any path except a perfect curve, the path a pendulum takes!

"And what is so characteristic of the pendulum? Why, the periods of vibration are the same! Do you think that knowledge didn't come in handy when I wanted to know *to the dot,* exactly when we'd reach the apex? You bet it did! And then there's something else about a pendulum —I'm surprised you didn't notice. At the Earth's pole the plane of vibration of a pendulum turns around once every twenty-four hours, in a direction opposite to that at which the Earth rotates. Rather, it appears that way. Actually, it is the Earth that turns around under the pendulum! And that's what happened to us. Didn't you notice that the stars as a whole never changed positions all during the time we were on the mirror? They didn't. We were a pendulum. The plane of our vibration was fixed in relation to space. This crazy planet revolved around under us because there wasn't any friction to say 'no'! So I figured it out diagrammatically—right! In my head! And if you think that wasn't a brain-twister—!

"I timed the first two or three vibrations after this pendulum stuff came up and hit me. I found each trip across took seventeen minutes, forty-five and four-tenths seconds. And I knew the period of rotation of this planet—fifty-two minutes, twenty-five and a fraction seconds. Notice anything about those figures, any general relation?"

"I get it," Colbie replied. He was sweating. His leg felt numb from the hip down. "One vibration took about one-third as long as the planet takes to make a revolution."

"Exactly! I'll keep talking, Colbie, help you forget the leg. And not only that, but the bottom of the mirror is a pole of the planet! So we were a true pendulum, vibrating at a planet's pole. And the length of our 'string,' the radius of the sphere, of which the mirror is a part, was out in space about sixteen hundred miles!

"Now in our vibrations, we always went through the

center of the mirror, but we never went across to the other side. That is, one swing always began and ended in one-half the mirror. In relation to space, our plane of vibration was always the same; in relation to the mirror, it was a curve which crept around the mirror, touching the rim six times.

"I had the devil of a time!" Deverel exclaimed. "I had to formulate a law which would tell me absolutely where each vibration would end, on the mirror, and thus how many times we'd have to swing across before we got back to our starting point—our original starting point. And finally I got this: One swing from rim to rim ends at that point on the rim which is opposite its starting point at end of swing. Get it? Well, if you don't, draw a diagram of a circle divided into six sixty-degree wedges—and follow the law out." And Colbie actually did draw such a diagram later. "In other words, it took us six swings from rim to rim to bring us back to our starting point. Those were the Crucial Moments. If we'd have got out at the wrong places, Colbie, we'd have starved before we traveled the distance back to the ships—if we knew where they were. Then, too, there was a chance one of us would end up pretty badly hurt! And one of us did—you had to drop back further than I'll have to.

"And that's all there is to it. I let you out at the end of the twenty-third trip from rim to rim. I'm getting out at the end of the twenty-fourth—what I really believe would have been the Final Crucial Moment. We couldn't have developed enough centrifugal force to send us over the rim if we'd gone around the mirror six more times, and fallen, as a consequence, sixty additional feet farther away from it. How's your leg?" he inquired.

"Rotten!" Colbie muffled a groan.

"Keep your chin up!" Deverel snapped. "Seven minutes and I'll be over the rim, and I'll hotfoot it back to the ships. It may take several hours before I get back here," he added in anxiety.

"I'll be all right," Colbie mumbled.

In the next few hours they kept in constant touch. Deverel made the rim, landed unharmed. He set off across the gouged plateau with both speed and care. He made the ships unharmed; and less than fifteen minutes later, the most beautiful sight in the world for Colbie was the sight of that slim, black IPF cruiser as it came zooming above Cyclops straight toward him.

It landed. Deverel stepped out. He picked Colbie up in his strong arms, carried him inside the ship, took off his spacesuit, and bared his broken leg. It was a simple facture, and was still in a healthy condition. Deverel went to work on it, put it in splints after having given it a wrench which accomplished the dual purpose of sending Colbie into a faint and setting the broken bone. Deverel put it in splints, and then bundled the IP man into bed.

Six weeks later, when Colbie was able to hobble around on a makeshift crutch, Deverel was still there.

"You make a nice nurse," Colbie told him over a meal one day. "Thanks—a lot."

"Skip it!" The outlaw grinned. "You weren't such a bad nurse yourself. I'd have been gone before now if you hadn't stepped in." He gulped a cup of coffee. "You're well enough, I figure," he said uneasily. " 'Bout time to go?"

Thoughtfully, uneasily, Colbie said, "Sure—I guess it is."

So that the next day Deverel sat down at the controls and touched them lightly. The ship shot upward into the eternal night of Cyclops, zoomed feather-light out over the strangest, most magical mirror ever to exist. And Colbie, looking at it, knew that he would always think of it with more affection than fear. He would always think of it as a child's colossal toy. It had so many amusing characteristics that he halfway felt it'd be a pleasure to go zooming down its infinitely smooth surface once again.

A dream world, he thought, if there ever was one.

Once landed near Colbie's ship, the outlaw said sardonically, "I guess we transfer from this ship to yours?"

Colbie met his eyes seriously for a moment, then got up from where he was sitting, and limped back and forth in the close confines of the cabin. His teeth were set, his eyes frowning, his fists opening and closing. He sat down again and got up. The look on his face was almost savage.

Suddenly he waved a hand violently, and a snarl contorted his features. He swung around, looking at the outlaw with hot, gray eyes. "I can't do it!" he snapped. He shoved out his jaw. "Not after what we've been through. Damn it, Deverel," he panted, "I don't like this job. I feel too friendly for you. I like you too damn much. You're a real guy. Hell, you could have run out any time you wanted to in the past six weeks.

"No. No, I can't do it. It'd be like"—he groped—"like taking unfair advantage, somehow. So," he said bitterly, "you're free." He forced a smile onto his face. "I'll write it in my report like this—'Captured outlaw, but he put one over on me and escaped.' "

"Right," Deverel agreed steadily.

"So I'll be going. I'll be here for, oh, about twenty-four hours. You going any place in particular?" he inquired politely.

"No-o-o," Deverel replied thoughtfully. "Don't know as I have any particular destination. Drop you a postcard? I will, if you think you need me for anything."

"Don't bother. I never have much trouble finding you," Colbie said airily. Then he put on a spacesuit. Deverel worked the valves, and a moment later Colbie stood in the air-lock. For a moment the two men stood there, saluting each other with grave eyes. Then the inner door closed and the outer opened.

Deverel watched Colbie enter his ship.

Then he sat down and, incandescent gases flaring from her stern jets, the slim cruiser accelerated until it was swallowed up in the trackless, illimitable wastes of space.

Astounding (November, 1938)
Swisher letter
Comment on *The Men and the Mirror*

Dear Mr. Campbell:

For some time now I have been considering Ross Rocklynne's story *The Men and the Mirror* in the July issue, but only the other night did I actually sit down with the figures given by Rocklynne (incidentally, that's the kind of story I appreciate . . . the author gives some actual data so that those who are interested can play around with a little arithmetic if they so desire). The results turned out to be quite amusing and interesting, to me at least, and they may be equally so to other readers.

As Rocklynne states, the two heroes (for they are certainly that, as it develops) constitute an isolated system, so that the various conservation laws must be obeyed, particularly the conservation of energy, of momentum and of angular momentum. The gentlemen, by their own exertions and manipulations, got themselves circling about each other at the ends of their two hundred foot rope so that, at the proper moment, when the rope was cut one flew up over the edge and the other received an equal impulse in the opposite direction to carry him over the opposite edge after traversing the mirror.

Momentum was conserved, since the two men flew apart in opposite directions, the momentum of one being exactly equal and opposite to that of the other. That presents no difficulty.

But angular momentum must also be conserved. The system of two men swinging in a circle at the ends of the rope represents considerable angular momentum, and the system must therefore contain in addition a precisely equal and opposite amount of angular momentum so that the total adds to zero. The only conceivable way this can be done seems to be with each man revolving on his own axis in a direction opposite to that of their orbital motion. In other words, if the two men are swinging clockwise on the ends of the rope, they must also be spinning counterclockwise each on his own longitudinal axis. How they accomplished this must be left to the imagination, aside from Rocklynne's description, in which he has them spinning each other like jo-jo's (we call them yo-yo's). He goes a step too far, however, in having them stop their spinning each on his own axis, since if they did that, their orbital motion on the ends of the rope must also necessarily have ceased.

Angular momentum is defined as the product of moment of inertia and angular velocity, just as linear momentum is the product of mass (or inertia) and linear velocity. So the moment of inertia of each man on his 100 foot radius, which we will call I, multiplied by his angular velocity, W, (the revolutions per minute, or radians per second traversed in their swinging about each other) must be equal to the moment of inertia of each man about his own longitudinal axis, i, multiplied by his angular velocity around that axis, w, or how fast he is spinning:

$$I W = i w.$$

Now we know that when the rope was cut, the man had

enough kinetic energy to throw him up 230 ft. to the rim of the mirror and 50 ft. beyond, or 280 ft., against the gravity of that world, 12 ft./sec². We shall assume for simplicity that each man weighs 100 kilos, or 220 lbs., slightly heavy, to be sure, except that they are in space suits. So the gentleman must have had kinetic energy of $220 \times 280 \times 12 = 740,000$ foot poundals, which we shall immediately transform to civilized metric units, 31,100 joules, or 3.11×10^{11} ergs. Thus his kinetic energy in his circular motion on the end of the rope is

$$\tfrac{1}{2} \text{ I } W^2 = 3.11 \times 10^{11} \text{ ergs.}$$

I is simply the mass of the man, 100,000 grams, times the square of his radius, 100 feet or 3048 centimeters, or

$$1 = 10^5 \times 3048^2 = 9.29 \times 10^{11} \text{ c.g.s. units.}$$

So we can solve for the angular velocity,

$W = \sqrt{.668} = .817$ radians per second, which is about 7.81 revolutions per minute. The angular momentum of each man about the center of the rope is then

$$\text{I W} = 9.29 \times 10^{11} \times .817 = 7.59 \times 10^{11} \text{ c.g.s.}$$
$$\text{units} = \text{i w.}$$

So if we knew the moment of inertia of a man about his longitudinal axis, i, we could figure how fast he is spinning on that axis, w. And that leads to the major difficulty —what is the moment of inertia of a man about his longitudinal axis? Needless to say, the equation of a man's surface would be pretty complicated in whatever coordinate system one wished to choose. But we can get an approximate answer by manufacturing several "men" with more regular and more easily handled shapes, and assume that the i of the ordinary 100 kilos man is around 1.45×10^7 c.g.s. units. The rest is duck soup:

$$\text{i w} = 1.45 \times 10^7 \text{ w} = 7.59 \times 10^{11}$$

$w = 5.23 \times 10^4$ radians per second, which is just about *500,000 revolutions per minute.* And so, if angular momentum is to be conserved, in order to build up a sufficient speed at the ends of the rope to throw the gentleman out of the mirror, each must revolve on his own axis some half a million revolutions per minute. It would take an agility nothing short of phenomenal to cut the rope at the correct time under such trying circumstances. And we do not wonder that a leg was broken in the fall to the ground, spinning at such an exorbitant rate. We are astonished only that the other leg was not worn down to a nub.

But that is not all! This spinning of the men about their own axes also represents kinetic energy, just as does their spinning about the center of the rope. How much? Simply

$$\frac{1}{2} \text{ I } w^2 = \frac{1.45 \times 10^7 \times 5.23^2 \times 10^5}{2} = 1.99 \times 10^{16} \text{ ergs.}$$

By conservation of energy, this must have been formed at the expense of the chemical energy of their bodies. Now an erg is not very much energy, but still the above number is quite large. This energy of spinning was imparted to themselves by their own muscular exertions during a period of less than 15 minutes, or 900 seconds. That means that each man must have been generating $\frac{1.99 \times 10^{16} \text{ ergs}}{900}$

per second during that 15 minutes, which represents a power of 2.21×10^6 joules per second, or 2210 kilowatts. For those who prefer the horse and buggy era, that is close to 3000 horsepower.

Saddest of all to the heroes must be the considering of their adventure in retrospect with the realization that if, instead of making all their acrobatic gyrations, they had merely pushed each other forcibly apart at the peak of their twenty-third trip across the mirror, projecting the one hero up 280 feet and the other one back over the other rim, if they could exert their gigantic push on each other over a period of 1 second, which does not seem too unreasonable, each man would only have to generate 3.11 × 10^{11} ergs in one second, which is 31 KW, or a little over 40 horsepower. So they could have accomplished the same results with only about one-seventieth the power applied over one second instead of 15 minutes, and with only .00156% the energy. That would have left them much less exhausted, not to mention the nausea from extreme dizziness.

And if they could devise some way of storing their energy, building it up over a period of 15 minutes but not building up the prohibitive rotational energy at the same time, they would only have needed $\frac{31}{900} = .0344$ KW or .0461 horsepower, which would be possible even for an ordinary man. It would be equivalent to climbing 105 feet, say up the stairway of an Earthly ten story building, in fifteen minutes.

From the above calculations we may conclude that although Rocklynne's method is physically quite possible, at least as far as the laws of mechanics are concerned, it would not be gymnastically possible for any but the most super of science-fiction heroes, those of the class which tends more to physical than mental agility.

But by all means do not take this as a condemnation of the story. I considered it quite good when I read it, and I still consider it so. It has provided not only the pleasure of reading, but added to that pleasure by presenting a little problem. By all means have more of the type.—Robert D. Swisher, 15 Ledyard Road, Winchester, Mass.

THEY FLY SO HIGH
(*Amazing Stories,* June 1952)

A fourth Colbie-Deverel was written after *The Men
and the Mirror* appeared. It was called *The Outlaw
Strider.* Mr. Campbell of *Astounding* quickly turned
it down and I agreed with him. I waited an excessively
long time before I rescued the scientific idea in the
story. I deliberately used the same formula, kept
"Colbie" under another name, and used a Gurdjieff-
like individual for the "outlaw"; then cut the story
to short story length. *They Fly So High* was supposed
to be the first story in a series of four (*Nearly Reach
the Sky, Then Like My Dreams, They Fade and Die*)
but this project died when I gave up writing for a
number of years.

Dornley, seated in the galley of the galloping spaceship
with his prisoner, was struck with a queer impression. Actually, Dr. Waldo Skutch was not worried that he had been
ousted at point of gun from Callisto.

"I could vacuum out another cup of coffee for you, sir"
—Dornley had been taught to be polite at the Space Academy, even to dangerous criminals—"but then you *don't*
seem to be nervous or worried, do you?" The best way
to get at the subject.

Besides, August Dornley felt he *did* have an inquiring
mind. Skutch, the authorities said, was planning the overthrow of the entire human race. Why? Where was his
criminal base located? What was the nature of the secret
arsenal of new weapons he was making? Good questions.
Find the answers. Get into Skutch's confidence.

"Nervous?" boomed Skutch, transfixing Dornley with

his pale strange eyes over which the cliffs of gray hair hung. "Worried? My dear young Lieutenant Dornley, worry is a special affection of the human race, an unnecessary evil of the mind for which they have great love. Worry is of the future; I, Skutch, am of the present." He touched his barrel-chest with a large, curved thumb.

"You don't consider yourself of the human race, sir?" This certainly was a question some clever interrogator would ask Skutch when he faced trial.

"I am of the human race; my physical body proves it, unfortunately. But as long as my mind functions, my chances of becoming unhuman are excellent, most excellent!" Skutch let go of his coffee cup to tap his great forehead, over which the disheveled coarse gray hair hung. "Brains, young man, brains. You are of the human race, and no doubt proud of it. But what have you done with your brains?"

Dornley would not let himself be irritated by this old man with the strange eyes. He smiled. "I got through the Space Academy in record time with top honors," he said. "If I hadn't had some kind of unusual merit, I would have been sent to the front lines in one of the warships. Instead, I was ranked up to Special Duty."

"And of that use of your brains you are proud!"

"Well, let's see," said Dornley, touched off a little. "I tracked you down to Callisto. I fooled you into leaving your ship. Then I set up a random-firing booby-gun, and caught you from behind. When it comes to a question of brains—"

Skutch threw back his great tattered head and laughed. His laughs were muted, gleeful squeals. Finally he stopped.

"Don't you think I knew I could not escape capture?" he demanded. "Now, let me ask you what happened to *your* ship."

110

Dornley's healthy tanned face showed a flush. "You blasted it," he admitted. "So what's the difference? We're using yours."

Skutch abruptly leaned across the table on his elbows, staring intently at Dornley. "You do have brains," he said in the gentlest tone he had used so far. "But you have not been taught to think. *Think,* young man, *think.* I, Skutch, do not worry about the future. But that does not mean that I do not consider the possibilities and the probabilities of the future. Now, can you *think?*"

Dornley was nettled at first. Then he felt distinct alarm. His training made him sit quietly, but it also made his hand inevitably grip the handle of his Biow thermo-gun.

"I'll make a guess," he said steadily. "This ship itself is a booby trap."

Suddenly he did get up, leaning his lank body over his chair to reach the galley vision disks. Jupiter showed one sweeping section of its baleful perimeter. He widened the aperture. Jupiter jumped back, showing itself in its entirety as a bulky, mottled orange. Around it stars lay thickly. Dornley rotated the pickup through one hundred and eighty degrees for all three coordinates. Japetus lay twenty minutes behind. The other satellites shone dimly.

Along the bottom of the disks, no pips of brilliance showed. There were no other ships in the area. Attack was ruled out, but so was the possibility of rescue.

He shut off the mechanism, faced Skutch quietly.

"So it's in the ship. Probably an explosive that you rigged into the fuel beforehand, primed to trigger off after a certain interval—unless you were free to unrig it." He could feel sweat trickling down his armpits. "I can also assume that there's nothing to be done about it at this late date, otherwise you wouldn't have tipped me off."

"Now," said Skutch, grinning widely, "you are think-

111

ing. But not enough. You really don't think I would ar-
range my own death. Actually, I would. My work is well
on its way. It is left in capable hands. I wouldn't be missed
for long. So I am prepared to let the ship blow up with
us in it if you do not move quickly."

Count to ten. Dornley said evenly, "You virtually admit
you are conspiring against humanity. This doesn't sound
very much like the idealized picture of yourself, Dr. Skutch,
as a superior human. Earth uses science to make war, a
war that is inevitable and must be fought. You plan to use
superior science to overcome both victor and loser. Is that
correct? Am I *thinking?*" He tossed the last out with bitter
sarcasm, then turned on his long legs and went aft fast.
He came back with two boxed pressure-suits, the supra-
lux type that would withstand, if necessary, fifteen thousand atmospheric pressures.

"You are thinking," said Skutch, frowning heavily at
him as he ripped open the boxes, "with the lower half of
your body."

Dornley, thin-lipped, ignored him utterly. Skutch rumbled on: "Science! Pah!" He almost spat. "Science is a toy,
a plaything. And I am a criminal because I desert my en-
forced task as toymaker. I am tracked down because it is
feared I am conspiring against authority. I am to be tried
and sentenced and forced to conceive of more ingenious
toys. Tried by men who are unconscious automatons, men
who think with the thoughts of others." He fell silent.

The boxes opened up; the pressure-suits came out, fat
dull things looking like blown-up corpses.

Skutch surveyed them interestedly. "Perhaps we do not
have enough time," he said gravely. "Will five minutes do?"

Dornley worked twice as fast, sweating, checking air
vents and controls, examining the pins of the gravity units,
making sure the food and water units were full and oper-

ating. Skutch observed this thoroughness with great approval.

"You can think," he said, nodding his great gray head. "But, here without a spirit of revenge motivating me, perhaps you have here an excellent example of how the free individual can manipulate the Universe. I, Skutch, am manipulating you, am manipulating this ship, am manipulating events—even though I am chained to this table. Wouldn't you give much for such an accomplishment?"

"I'd give much if you'd shut up, Dr. Skutch," Dornley said firmly. Skutch shrugged his heavy old shoulders. "Now, get into this suit."

Dornley unchained him and helped him in, bolting down the solid, transparent supra-lux visor. Skutch choked a little. Dornley readjusted the intake of oxygen. Thirty-nine seconds later they shot out from the air-lock and Skutch, handcuffed to Dornley, was dryly complimenting him for a fast piece of work. Ten seconds later, several large cracks abruptly appeared in the slim black ship's hull. Through these cracks, and through the shattered ports, was seen a glow of fuming violence. Bilious yellow gases escaped under pressure, swiftly expanded to the point of invisibility. The numerous cracks in the hull became a little larger, that was all. They began moving, under their own velocity, farther and farther away until the derelict was gone.

Dornley was depressed and silent. Actually, he could blame himself and a certain amount of inexperience for having fallen into a trap. Skutch was a wise old bear; and, it appeared, he understood human nature. Looking down at giant Jupiter—that immense planet did determine where *down* was—he was almost sure it would have been better to take a quick death in the ship.

"Jupiter," mused Skutch. His voice came through the

radio receiver with its booming quality strained out. "Jupiter, giant of the system, a mighty creature, an aged old man. Jupiter, my friend, I salute you. Soon we shall meet."

Dornley said nothing. Skutch said, "You did not know, I suppose, that Jupiter is alive?"

Dornley turned his head until his face was against Skutch's. He was sure he was looking at a crazy old man. But Skutch grinned hugely, his gray whiskers protruding around his mouth like those of a tiger.

"I have trapped you, young man. You are, it would appear, much worse off than I expected. You would make the statement, flatly, that Jupiter does *not* live. Your mind is fettered. You are chained to dogma. Other minds tell you what to think. Perhaps I should discard you." He sighed heavily, but calculatingly.

Dornley said flatly, "Jupiter is *not* alive."

"You see?" Skutch's free arm appealed to the cold stars. "If only he had said 'I do not have sufficient material on which to base an opinion. Jupiter *may* be alive.'"

Dornley smiled wanly. "Men have landed on Jupiter. They've built Jupiter City up near the Red Spot. They haven't detected a heartbeat, or breathing. But I'll grant you the point. He might be alive in other ways."

"Good, good," applauded Skutch. "You are showing signs of improvement. Understand me, young man. Sometimes I make flat statements which I do not know to be true. But these are merely for testing people."

"Which people?"

"*All* people," said Skutch solemnly. "I have my life work which you do not yet know about. I am, you would say at your present level of understanding, creating an ultimate weapon, a weapon so powerful that none will stand against it. For this I would be damned, sentenced to

114

death if the Terrestrial Court ever got hold of me, which they shall not. We are falling now."

They were indeed falling. The planet's powerful drag had finally overcome their momentum outward; the meter in the wrist of Dornley's pressure-suit, accurately judging the changing shifts of satellite and planetary gravities, gave them an accelerating velocity. They would, at this rate, hit the planet's atmosphere in eight hours. No good. Every hour, at least, they would have to adjust the gravity units built into the suits to cut their speed down.

Dornley, attached to his strange companion, stared down at that broad orange, yellow, and red monster of the sky. Vagrant fear-thoughts floated to the surface of his mind. He knew he should be screaming with terror. They were alone out here, detached from things, living with a finality equal to death. His heart beat a little faster; his breathing stepped up. He began to think of himself as still a young punk, with a long and satisfactory life not yet ready to be cut short. He sweated.

"Dr. Skutch," he said hoarsely, "how do you do it? Why aren't you afraid?"

"Afraid?" Skutch's voice was astonished. Then it became very soft and gentle. "I understand, young man," he said. "You are worried. You think we will not live. And why is this?"

The question was gently probing.

Dornley bit his lip. "It's obvious. Jupiter has caught people before. Ships unable to fight free of the gravity. They've sent distress signals that were picked up. No rescue ship could get to them in time. And we don't even have sending equipment."

"Aha!" Skutch's teeth clicked triumphantly. "We come to the core of mankind's woes. Man looks back on past

115

occurrences, and plans the future accordingly. The future therefore is thought of as a carbon copy of the past. This is definitely not so, young man. Your no doubt excellent brain is using identity thought. What a dangerous thing! Understand this: *no one* event is identical with another. What is happening to us now has no relationship whatever with anything that ever happened to anybody else. This is a new situation. We can make of it what we will without letting past events dictate to us. Do you understand?"

"It makes sense," Dornley said wearily. "But it still scares the living daylights out of me."

"My dear Lieutenant Dornley," Skutch snapped with asperity, "that is because you are, if I may say it, not alive. You are not *being*. Look around you!" He made a great, enthusiastic, sweeping arc with his free arm. "Would you be dead like most of mankind? Here you have beauty! Here you have majesty! Here you have depth and mystery and awesome ideas to contend with! There is joy out here, not terror. Young man, I command you *to be!*"

If there had been anything to sit on, Dornley would have sat up at the sternness in Skutch's voice. At any rate, he felt some kind of bells ringing in his head, and he did look around. It was beautiful, he decided forlornly—if you didn't worry.

Skutch was looking through Dornley's visor at him. He grinned widely. "That's better. Young man, I have a suggestion. Go to sleep. I shall be sure to adjust our falling speed so that we shall not strike the atmosphere fast enough to create heat."

Dornley did go to sleep, as if Skutch had used positive suggestion. He slept long, solidly, and potently. When he awoke, it was because he and Skutch were pinwheeling through a thickening atmosphere. Skutch muttered something about not knowing where the stabilizer controls were. Dornley found them for him; soon, the tiny gyroscopes whirring, they were falling feet first.

There was little light. Starlight could not penetrate this incredibly thick skin of gases that covered Jupiter. A red glow, originating from the reflection of the Great Red Spot halfway around the planet, afforded hardly any illumination. Dornley turned on the search-beam unit in the breast of his suit to read his meters. Twelve hundred miles to go to get to the surface. He spoke to Skutch. Skutch muttered groggily. Dornley said nothing more, and let Skutch fall asleep.

The vigil could have been full of terror, but Dornley reflected that some of Skutch's strange philosophy had gotten through to him, and no doubt would keep him pepped up for a while. He frowned. A strange experience, a strange man, who *was* working on an ultimate weapon, and *did* have conspirators working with him, by his own admission.

Something didn't jibe. What? No answer.

They fell. Dornley thought, so this was a new situation? Hm-m-m. But it was the same deadly planet. But maybe not. Old Man Jupiter was a guy with many faces, many mysteries, ninety-nine percent unknown.

Two and a half times Earth gravity; fifteen thousand times Earth's atmospheric pressure!

Dornley grimaced down through heaving blackness. "Jupiter, old man," he prayed as an experiment, "let us down easy. And if we get away free, and I get Skutch where he belongs, I promise . . ." *Could go to church every Sunday; but Jupiter doesn't care.*

Five hundred miles. Dornley didn't dare take his eyes away from the set of meters. One hundred miles. He kept his eyes glued to them. Ten miles. He tried to wake up Skutch. Two miles. Skutch would not waken. One thousand feet.

"Skutch!" screamed Dornley. Three hundred feet. But fractional readings didn't work. Twenty-five feet below his search-beam glanced off a liquid, gleaming surface. Dornley, robbed of the time to do things properly, wasn't able to throw Skutch's gravity reactor over; he could only shove over his own. Result, not enough gravity decrease. They hit hard and went under.

Under

Thank you, Old Man Jupiter.

Skutch was muttering as they floated up. Floated up was not the best description of the process. They were being carried up. Nor did they break surface. The surface was under them.

In any event, the movement ceased. Dornley's chest-beam was still on. It illuminated what at first glance seemed to be a smooth circular cavern exuding a greenish, a gorgeous radiance. The radiance was, of course, the dispersed radiance of the beam.

Skutch muttered again. Dornley tried to move. He was flat on his back, locked tight against Skutch. Like a vise. His helmet was held down; he could barely move his head inside it. One arm was lying free against his chest; he carefully kept it that way. His legs were clamped together, and in turn locked to Skutch's. His other arm was squeezed in tight to Skutch's. Strange.

Silence. Skutch spoke. "Well, young man? You are thinking?"

Dornley *was* thinking—rather detachedly. He was thinking of two men alone on an uninhabited planet—uninhabited except for an inaccessible domed city halfway around the planet. Two men thinking of impossibilities, in terms of hope and escape and rescue.

So he should think. What he should do was reach over with his free arm and tune the great Dr. Waldo Skutch's oxygen intake to zero.

Skutch's sigh came. "I am disappointed in you, Lieutenant. An unchained mind already would have diagnosed the situation and be devising solutions. The free man manipulates the world; the world manipulates the slave. Are you slave to your own pessimism? That is the important problem, not whether you will continue to live.

"However, I shall start your enslaved mind to working. The 'cave,' as you have already misnomered it, is not a cave. Listen to the Jupiter wind." A wind did sound, outside somewhere, a whining, gusty thunder that rose, fell, augmented, diminished. The gorgeously green "cave" expanded and contracted correspondingly, sometimes as much as two or three feet.

"You see?" Skutch chuckled. "Jupiter is breathing. We have fallen into his mouth and are enveloped in a bubble of spit! One's imagination could make much of this. But let us stick to fact, fact at least as the mind of man knows it.

"Fifteen thousand atmospheres press on a lake of strange liquid metal. A unique distortion occurs on the surface of the lake. One could say that a surface tension thousands of times one would think possible is almost certain to be created. *Now* you are thinking?" Skutch's voice was hopeful; he was like a man who has primed a pump and is sure water must come out.

"Hell," muttered Dornley rebelliously. He was thinking of two needles locked together on a surface film of water. So how does one free the two needles so they can

119

eddy around for a while with a certain amount of freedom? Stir up the water around them, maybe. Not that exactly. . . .

"Don't worry, I'm not exactly dead," he told Skutch. "I've got a free arm. I've also got an idea."

He could reach Skutch's gravity unit rheostat with some effort; his own was easy. He turned both rheostats on full; instantly, their weights increased and they sagged below the surface of the liquid stuff, lying in a sort of deep hollow.

"Get set," he told Skutch. He turned both rheostats suddenly back to the zero mark, which equaled one-half a gravity. Dornley's breath whooshed out as the sag in the surface of the lake bounced back in place, snapping the two men a half dozen feet into the air.

There was a breaking sound. When Dornley came to, he was sitting cross-legged a half dozen feet from Skutch. Skutch had fallen on his back, helpless again, arms and legs forced together. But he was chuckling delightedly, and told Dornley that when he came this way, he could pull Skutch to a sitting position too.

Dornley was about to demonstrate that he intended to stay where he was when he noticed that inevitably the strengthened surface between them was drawing them together. Well, anyway, the handcuffs, brittle in the subzero cold, had snapped, and Dornley was arm-free, so there was that much gained.

A moment later, the two men were sitting knee to knee.

Dornley now looked around with greater interest.

"It's a bubble, all right," he admitted. "Big babies. There's a gas seepage in the bed of the lake, I'd say. The wind causes change in pressure outside. That's a good aerodynamic principle that works on any planet. The bubble gets bigger or smaller accordingly."

Latest U.S. Government
tests of all cigarettes
show True is
lower in both
tar and nicotine
than 98% of all other
cigarettes sold.

Think about it.
Shouldn't your next cigarette be True?

Regular: 12 mg. "tar", 0.8 mg. nicotine,
Menthol: 12 mg. "tar", 0.7 mg. nicotine, av. per cigarette, FTC Report Aug. '72.

Latest U.S. Government
tests of all menthol
cigarettes show
True is lower
in both tar and
nicotine than 98% of
all other menthols sold.

Think about it.
Shouldn't your next cigarette be True?

© Lorillard 1973

Warning: The Surgeon General Has Determined
That Cigarette Smoking Is Dangerous to Your Health.

One section of the bubble became a flat wall.

"Interesting," commented Dornley, so fascinated he didn't know his worry about the future had momentarily slipped away. "Another bigger bubble bumped into it."

Skutch surveyed him with an extremely friendly smile, but he said nothing, being speechless for the first time.

Dornley tentatively tugged his Biow thermo-gun from its holster, and after some hesitation took a potshot at the two bubbles' connecting skin. It turned a brighter green in one spot, but didn't break, so Dornley turned the temperature up a little. This time there was a crack of thunder, and things happened. Dornley and Skutch were tossed around, and when things quieted down, they were again being forced together, and a bubble four times as big arched over them. The two bubbles apparently had merged.

Dornley grinned, and Skutch grinned back.

"You see?" Skutch spread his hands as if life itself had been explained. "One plays with toys, but one does not allow toys to play with him—unless he wants them to. In this way, free men master all that is within and without them. Now, my dear Lieutenant, I am sure you have determined our next step, the means of securing escape from this lake?" His shaggy brows went up.

Dornley surveyed him thoughtfully. He was beginning to get certain ideas, very strong and intuitive ideas.

"I have not determined it," he stated.

The shaggy face behind the visor smiled broadly. Skutch reached out a hand. "Let me have your gun, young man," he commanded.

Instead of doing that, Dornley brought the gun up and centered it on the chest of Skutch's pressure-suit.

He said conversationally, "Dr. Skutch, if I were to turn the heat intensity on this thermal weapon up, to full blast,

121

it would take me five minutes to burn a hole in your suit and let fifteen thousand atmospheric pressures in."

Skutch's face was wrenched with a bitter surprise. He snarled. *"Why?"*

"I've been a good boy, Dr. Skutch. I didn't lose my temper when you began . . . uh . . . manipulating me. I treated you like a prisoner of war, with courtesy, with great courtesy. Believe me, I shall continue to be courteous. But I am still a member of the Service, and I have my duty. We are *not* friends."

Skutch relaxed visibly, his tiger-look vanishing. "Oh, that." He shrugged contemptuously. "Duty. Courtesy. Catchwords. Other men's thoughts again. They mean nothing."

"That's not all," said Dornley determinedly. "I have certain beliefs regarding you. One is that you *are* conspiring to overthrow not only the Earth government, but the governments, eventually, of the other planets as well. The enemy planets."

"Enemy!" Skutch raised his hands to invisible gods. "There he goes again! Whose enemy? Not his enemy. The enemy of the higher-ups who think for him. You have learned nothing from me, young man, *nothing?*"

Dornley felt his thinking apparatus going haywire.

"Furthermore," he went on distractedly, "you *do* have a base, a headquarters, and you have many men under you. This has been suspected too. But not until now has anyone been convinced of its location. That base, I am convinced, is on this planet. And not too far from here! Else, *why* are you so optimistic?

"Again, by your own admission to me, you, a genius in the field of science, are working with your men on a weapon so powerful that it could not be withstood by any power. Of this I believe you are capable.

"Dr. Skutch, I can be optimistic too, under certain conditions, but I *know* we can't reach Jupiter City. And I cannot allow you the possibility of escape to your headquarters, even if I die.

"I am sure I should kill you now."

Skutch grunted. "Why don't you?"

Dornley sweated. Skutch grunted again, almost disinterestedly. "You don't believe half of what you're saying, Lieutenant. That's why. You're waiting for proof from me. I'll give you proof. My base *is* near here—only three thousand miles. You do think. And I do have many men—and women—and children—under me. And I am creating a super-weapon that is intended to destroy! Tell me, Lieutenant, how would you like to see that super-weapon in operation?"

Dornley clamped his teeth together. "I would, but—"

"Excellent!" Some of Skutch's ebullience came back. Then his stare became bright and penetrating.

"Lieutenant, what possessions do you have?"

The direction of the conversation was going out of control. Dornley felt loggy. "None," he said wearily. "I'm in the Service. A few papers, old letters, some civilian clothes, a number of books. That's all. Why?"

"You're not married? You have no children? You have no relatives you are tied to?" At Dornley's lack of replies in the affirmative, he cried, "Excellent, excellent, excellent! Lieutenant, how would you like to take a trip to my base, my so-called militant headquarters, and watch the rays of my deadly weapon at work?"

Dornley felt himself crumbling. He suspected some kind of equivocation here that would put him in a still worse position. But worse from whose viewpoint? He was tired of thinking. Well, answer the question. From the viewpoint of duty, from the viewpoint of oaths, from the viewpoint of the men who bossed the men who bossed the men who bossed the men, who in turn got their ideas and their convictions from official papers written by the last generation, or men ten generations dead, who had written books and conceived traditions and rules. . . . A tanglework of convention and protocol and axiomatic falsehoods that had a bad beginning. War, poverty, pain, violence, science, more science, better science, super-science, war, poverty. . . . Super-dooper science. . . .

Pensively he looked beyond Skutch. Life was wrong. Yes, drastically wrong somehow. He was in a position where he should kill Skutch—but he couldn't. What then? He had to go with Skutch. That too was being forced on him. Go with Skutch! Find out, at least, what he was up to. Get a look at this so-called super-weapon, at his base, at the people he worked with. And then—

He shook his head regretfully. "I can't kill you, Doctor. I'll go with you, if we can make it. If I don't like what I see, I promise I'll leave and won't say anything. That goes against my oath, but that's the way I'll stand."

"But if you do like it?" The question was probing.

"You'd want me to stay? Give up Earth?"

"Bah!" Skutch rocked back. "You never had Earth. Earth had you. No, no, young man. You'd go back. Someday we'll all go back—if we want to. But not for long."

Dornley gave him a fleeting, worn smile, said nothing. Skutch's breath came out in a long, sustained sigh.

Dornley looked at his gun. "As for getting to 'dry' land," he mused, "that should be easy. A spot heat should reduce the tension and give us a pull in the opposite direction."

He destroyed the gently vibrating bubble with a single blast. It disappeared in thunder, though for a second great drops of it rained down. Dornley waited until he and

Skutch once more swung together, waited until he had accustomed himself to winds that had the push of under-sea currents. He then adjusted the gun to maximum aperture. This gave him a fanning beam, which he played on the surface film to his left, adequately lessening its tension.

The surface forces to Dornley's right being greater, they contracted continuously, pulling him and Skutch smoothly away from the heated surface. Dornley, wanting to be sure they did not move in a circle, turned up the stabilizers.

After an hour, what would roughly be described as a "beach" appeared. Strong cohesive forces, however, caused the lake edge to sweep upward in a sharp curve, a dozen feet high. Dornley surveyed that obstacle distrustfully, but apparently the strength of the contracting film was enough to overcome gravitational pull. They swooped up, poised. Skutch clawed at the rocky ledge of the beach and got free. Dornley was poised on the lip. Skutch got him under the armpits and heaved him out.

Dornley looked questioningly at Skutch as they stood free with ammonia-methane winds moving sluggishly around them. Skutch motioned him to sit down.

"They'll come for us," he said complacently.

"They know we're here?" Dornley was incredulous.

Skutch grinned hugely. "Why not? Science is not an end, but it is a tool." He picked up two slate-colored rocks, knocked them together. "Sounds travel, and do not stop. Instruments pick up vibrations. They'll be here. We do have ways to move about the planet."

There was silence. Then Dornley saw that Skutch was looking at him, intently, purposefully.

"You will live with us," Skutch said slowly. "You will learn. There will be girls there. There will be girls who will fall in love with you—if they want to. You will lack for nothing. But you must learn.

"When I say Jupiter is alive, you will say maybe it is alive, and try to find out why I think it is alive. When I say apple trees will thrive in a glass of water, you will question the concept. You will reexamine every tradition, every convention, every idea that has been thrust at you and which you have been forced to accept. You will ask why you *must* do such and such. Who said so? You will begin throwing out hundreds of false ideas, but *you* will use *them,* they will not use you. You will examine your fears, your guilts, your jealousies, your envies. Eventually, you will compel them, they will not compel you. No thing, no one, no idea, will ever use you again. Unless you want it to."

He rocked back on his haunches, hands on his spread knees, grinning his tiger's grin.

"The prospect frightens you? Do not let it, young man. Already I have used my secret weapon on you. Its rays are deeply imbedded in your body. Already you see how easily one's own personal bubbles can burst. You will never be the same.

"But not for a thousand years will we, or those who come after us, be ready for humanity itself."

The winds moved sluggishly. Time passed. Dornley sat stricken, wondering what he could discard, wondering what he could keep.

THE BOTTLED MEN
(*Astounding Science Fiction,* June 1946)

The story is Colbie-Deverel all over again, but I changed the names to protect the pages of *Astounding*. At least so I thought. The stories seemed to be from another era, not suited to the magazine's progression into better characterization and perhaps more mature plotting. With new characters I could produce side elements of conflict and do some whimsical stuff with characterization in the person of a lighthearted fake of a villain named Gull Norse. Looking back, however, it may not have been too much of a trick to bow to the tradition and accede to the nostalgic yearnings of the many science fiction fans who asked about my Colbie-Deverels. Revealingly enough, two years ago, thirty years after the last one, I started another Colbie-Deverel. Started, that's all: We all make trips back to our childhood.

The elevator doors slid open. A tall man, trimly garbed in the gray-edged black uniform that was the habiliment of members of the Solar Guard, stepped into the room. He looked around for a second with patient gray eyes, then moved lightly toward "Uncle Jim" Post's desk. Uncle Jim, referred to thus by his millions of subordinates, was the supreme commander of the SAG—Solar System Associated Guard.

"At ease, Lieutenant," said Post, as the black uniformed man drew himself to attention.

Lieutenant Marc Sturm relaxed. He said politely, "I was requested to report to you at this time, sir."

"Yes, Lieutenant. Lieutenant, your application for marriage has been rejected."

"Yes, sir." Sturm showed no reaction.

"Do you have any objection to raise?"

"Yes, sir. I believe the Control Council's decision unfair."

"It's not unfair if the human race expects to make the progress charted out for itself."

Sturm said nothing. Post squirmed a little, as if with repressed rage at Sturm's silence. Post was tall, bony, hawk-nosed, with blue eyes that could be kind. In the silence, he let his eyes wander toward the window. Outside, the high traffic lanes swarmed with twenty-fifth century cars. An occasional rocket ship, or jet-propelled planet car moved through the violet-blue atmosphere. This was Satterfield City on the planet Mars—a Mars that had been partially rehabilitated by the human race.

Post's eyes came back, dropped to the eugenics application on his desk. He raised a corner of the form. He said:

"Lieutenant, you have a right to know the exact reason for the rejection. Your psychological portrait, as prepared by the Control Council reads .8w-.7p-.2c-.5g-.5f. I think you must know that portrait by heart. I think you must also know Lieutenant Colonel Susan Quincy's portrait by heart and realize that they don't dovetail."

There was something challenging in his voice.

Sturm's face was expressionless. For the first time, he volunteered a question. "May I ask why the Control Council gave the ultimate decision for the rejection into your hands, instead of dealing with me direct?"

Post smiled. "You may. I wanted you to ask that question. The fact is, there was a shred of doubt in the minds of the Council. Namely, that in some respects your psychological portrait and that of Susan's do have some

128

items which dovetail. You're both .8w's for instance, which is good. And there's a divergence of only .3 in 'p,' the factor of rigidity—in your favor. Which is as it should be in a marriage, I suppose. However, the rejection still stands, Lieutenant."

His eyes averted. "The fact is, Lieutenant, Lieutenant Colonel Susan Quincy outranks you."

Sturm's sudden agitation was betrayed only by the rubbing of the fingers of both hands across each other. He said, "I don't understand what that would have to do with it, sir."

"It has everything to do with it. Susan's prestige for instance. She's the commander of the Woman's Martian Police Corps, you know. We can't have the commander of the WMPC married to a man who'll never go beyond the rank of second lieutenant."

The bomb that Post knew he had to throw exploded somewhere deep among the recesses of Sturm's mind. No slightest flash or sound of the explosion came back. Sturm stood there, wooden-faced.

Post squirmed again, as if with controlled rage. He said, "Man, don't you have *anything* to say for yourself?"

Sturm said, "I understand that your point-blank statement that I'll never rise above my present rank arises from my failure to capture Gull Norse last week, when I practically had him in my hands."

"That's partly it. But your failure to capture Gull is merely a result of your faulty psychological pattern."

"I beg to differ with your statement." Sturm's voice was soft and polite. "I haven't failed to capture Gull Norse."

"You haven't?" Post raised an ironic eyebrow.

"No. His capture by me is merely postponed. Gull Norse is still my assignment. I expect to make his arrest in anywhere from one to four weeks."

For the first time, Sturm appeared to lose his remarkable composure. He bit at his lower lip, blinked rapidly. His slowly rubbing fingers balled up into half-fists.

"I also want to differ with the Control Council on that . . . that psychological portrait of mine. Mathematical symbols can't take into account every factor of character, sir. I don't disagree with what the portrait does tell. It's what it leaves out. .8w., character integration, is good, and sets me up as a pretty sound citizen. .2c, the factor of extraversion, points me out as pretty much of a poor mixer, not very sociable, not very good at small talk or quick on the uptake. .5g isn't good either, because it indicates a general mental capacity about .3 below Susan's . . . pardon me; below Lieutenant Colonel Quincy's. In other words, just an average intelligence. .5f indicates a certain neuroticism—I guess I do show signs of being neurotic, because if I weren't, I wouldn't repress myself in front of you and I'd blow my top."

Post's blue eyes closed a little, became quizzically enigmatic. He leaned back in his chair. "Go on, Lieutenant."

Sturm's words came a little faster, a little harder. "I left the rigidity factor out till last, sir. I've got a .7p rigidity, sir. That's what I mean when I say the Council can't put everything into symbols. They can't put into symbols the four years I spent at Decimal Point—" Decimal Point was the popular name for Marto-Tellurian Spatial Academy. "They can't explain by symbols why, if I'm so stupid, I came out with third highest honors in my class."

Post's voice was oddly muffled. "I'm not sure I knew that, Lieutenant. Please go on."

Sturm's hands were fists now. "Don't think I wasn't conscious of the general inferiority of my 'g' rating during those years at the Point. Other cadets breezed through their exams without hardly glancing at a book. I had to bone up for hours—even days, and all night. But when the grades were handed out, I came out on top, generally. I'm pointing out that the factor of rigidity includes the general mental pattern of the ability to work—and to fight too—and a sort of dogged, stupid perseverance that doesn't know when to give up. That's why I think the Council is way off. They don't understand those four years of mine at Decimal Point, and they don't understand that what I don't get by brainwork I get by a bulldog stick-to-it-tive-ness."

He paused. His full lips curled slightly, just a shade toward insulting insubordination. "I don't suppose you'll understand it either."

Post blinked. He came erect. His voice was quick. "On the contrary! I do understand." His eyes twinkled. "Are you being persevering now?"

"Yes, sir. I intend to marry Susan."

"Oh-ho!" Post's eyebrow was ironic again. "Your analysis of your own portrait doesn't particularly change it, you know. Just makes it a little clearer. My objections still stand."

He was watching Sturm closely.

Sturm's eyes became patient again, without a trace of humor. "After I bring Gull Norse in, sir, I'll automatically receive a raise in rank."

"From whom?"

"From you, sir. Having received a raise in rank, I don't feel you'll stand in the way of our marriage."

Post grinned widely, then laughed outright. "Lieutenant, you amaze me with your calm assumptions. But I'll tell you what." His hand slapped the desk. "It's a deal! You'll jump to a captaincy and you can marry Susan—*if* you bring Gull in."

"When I bring him in, sir. Which will be sometime in the next month, probably sooner. Is that all, sir?"

"What else is there?" Post's smile was wry. "You've gained everything you wanted from this interview, haven't you? Good day, Lieutenant."

"Good day, sir."

Sturm saluted smartly, turned, and shortly the elevator swallowed him up again.

Post sat still for a moment, musing, then reached out and pressed a series of buttons on his desk. Shortly, a buzzer sounded, and Post scooped up the radio-phone.

"Susan—Uncle Jim. Yes, I just spoke with him, and I did everything I could. I insulted him—not that the insults weren't rooted in clear, cold fact. I'm sorry, my dear, but those symbols *do* tell a lot. Anyway, he's determined to bring Gull in, and I hope he can swing it, for your sake. But it's a tough deal, and my personal feelings are that with a man like Gull, an excess of 'p' isn't going to make up for a lack of 'g.'"

In the elevator, Second Lieutenant Marc Sturm had a very different expression than the one he had showed Uncle Jim Post. It was a hangdog, suffering expression, as if he had been beaten with whips. Or as if a corps of psychiatrists had been grilling him to detect traces of insanity. He felt completely muddled inside. He was never more ready to give up in his life than when Post had, point-blank, come out with the bad news. Something had made him hang on—the same something that made him hang on when he knew he was going to fail a semester at Decimal Point. Or the same something that had made it possible for him to attain the rank of second lieutenant.

His face was under control again when he stepped smartly from the elevator. He went with brisk step toward the transparent sheet of light which served as a door to the street outside. He was just about to step through when somebody tapped him on the shoulder. He turned, frowning. A little man with tortoise-rimmed glasses, and dressed in a baggy suit, grinned at him.

"Lieutenant, this is luck!" His voice was rapid, reedy. "I've been hunting for a story for the Satterfield *Times*. I says to myself, man, if only I could run across that Second Lieutenant Marc Sturm. I could get a couple paragraphs out of him about how the big bad man of space Gull Norse walked away from him one evening last week without so much as a gunshot."

Marc Sturm's impulse was to grab the scrawny throat and choke the life out of it. He said in a very polite tone, "I'm sorry. I have nothing more to add to that story. Good day."

The man said, sardonically touching his hand to his hat, "OK, soldier-boy. Don't blame you. I'd try to kill publicity on that myself."

Marc had already turned away, gone through the door. Just outside the door, street-noises around him, he stopped, hot eyes closed. Then something clicked. He went back inside, found the reporter standing in front of one of the elevators.

Marc said, stopping before him, "Pardon me. I can give you a few lines. Quote: Questioned by reporters, Lieutenant Marc Sturm today expressed surprise that most of the comments of the newspapers on the matter of the escape of Gull Norse from his hands indicate that Gull's escape is a permanent affair. Sturm said, 'The comments mostly indicate the stupidity of the managing editors who allowed the stories to be published. I am unable to make my plans public knowledge, but in anywhere from one to four weeks, Gull Norse will be in the hands of the law.'

"Sturm added: 'If anyone cares to look into my record, he may do so. I've never pitted myself against an outlaw of Norse's type. On the other hand, I've never failed to bring in any man. Either dead or alive. I'll probably be forced to bring Gull in dead.' Sturm looked in good spirits, and was completely unabashed about charges which described the Gull Norse escape a result of his stupidity. End quote. Did you get that?"

"Every word," the reporter said, with a bored yawn. He turned away. "I'll try to give you a paragraph or two, soldier-boy," he said, indulgently. "Better look out for Gull Norse, though. He probably won't like that threat to bring him in dead."

The next day, Marc Sturm left his quarters in full uniform, and caught the monorail for Solar Guard Depot, where they had his two-man patrol ship in readiness to "hit heaven." On the way, he bought the Satterfield *Times*. On page 2 he found the story, very surprisingly reproduced word for word. A couple of paragraphs had been added:

Sturm's boast was made as a result of his bungling effort to bring one of the most feared criminals in the System under the wings of the law last Wednesday. Sturm, sometimes referred to as the fearless second lieutenant, captured Gull in a joy-joint when Gull was supposedly drunk. Sturm fell for the dodge, but Gull feigned intoxication for the purpose of making Sturm relax his guard. Gull broke loose, making an easy getaway.

Sturm's previous record shows that most of his assignments dealt with petty lawbreakers, most of whom, it is admitted, were under the influence of liquor.

Sturm's big hands crumpled the paper with a slow crunching motion. *One for the scrapbook,* he thought bitterly. Yet he had expected no less.

Second Lieutenant Marc Sturm left the planet Mars in his two-man patrol boat on Sol 2, Hour 21, Martian Equatorial Time. He preferred not to blast around the Sun on a triple straight-angle, but instead chose a slow Hohman curve for the first part of his trip.

He had brought certain equipment along with him. It was part of a plan he had formulated over a period of time. For several days, he did an intricate wiring job beneath the bulkheads, and installed several sets of an equally intricate pattern of tubes and inductance coils throughout the rear of the ship. He laid wires under the deck plates to his instrument board in the partly transparent nose of the ship. He attached these to a small switchboard set facedown in the control panel.

On the third day he was finished, and bolted all plates back into place. He then took a case of canned goods, placed it on the floor at the rear of the ship. He went forward, flipped on the finger-switch. Instantly, there was an electric tension in the air, felt this far forward so strongly that every hair on Sturm's body pointed toward the locus of the force-field. The case of canned goods at the same moment jumped up from the deck plates violently and remained suspended in the air at the center of the force-field, slowly rotating.

Sturm smiled, and as the ship crawled through the cosmic emptiness at a snail's pace he tried the stunt over and over again, securing a pleasurable sensation from imagining that it was Gull Norse who hung there so helplessly.

He tired of his Hohman curve, now, which wasn't

getting him any place, but had allowed him to leave the controls for several hours at a time. He poured the power on, slipped into a straight angle trajectory, and in days to follow skirted the very edge of the Sun's "boiling zone," then left the Sun behind.

As the Sun's girth began to diminish with distance, he often quartered his vision plate, taking a sternward view of the cosmos. He swept every tiniest segment of sky to the rear, hoping to pick up a telltale exhaust, indicating he was being followed. He saw no such sign; which of course meant nothing. The pursuing ship, if there was one, might be using the new spot-jet method of propulsion.

He passed Mercury's orbit, then set up a mass-detector which would enable him to find the tiny, errant asteroid on which he intended to land.

He found it soon enough, and almost ten days after leaving Mars, landed.

The landing was not a conventional affair. To anyone watching, it was very apparently a forced, not an intended landing. A flaring, explosive burst of vapors leaped from the pilot blast of the ship on the starboard side. The little ship spun madly in space, then made a few feeble tries at turning her nose toward the asteroid only a few thousand miles away. It did make headway, finally landed broadside on, with only a few minor jars and bumps.

After Sturm accomplished the deception—by adding a few grams of *d-c-tonite* to the starboard pilot blast—he leaned back and lighted a cigarette. The stage had been set. He could only hope that one of the chief characters had been in the audience, and would soon enter to speak his lines.

Not far out in space, one of the new spot-jet ships hung

moveless. For several hours the occupant of the ship had been studying the activities of the moving figure down on the asteroid. The figure was apparently dismantling a fused pilot blast, inserting a spare.

The figure now went inside the ship, leaving the outer door of the air-lock open. The man watching these activities uttered an exclamation, got the spot-jet ship into furious motion, and in ten or fifteen seconds flat had completed a great circle which put it on the other side of the asteroid.

At the same swift pace, it hurtled along a few feet above the surface of the asteroid, landed about ten feet from the Solar Guard patrol ship. The hatchway opened and a big man got hurriedly out. He ran toward the Solar Guard ship, his fifteen-pound flame pistol hanging from his gauntleted fingers. He went straight through the outer door of the air-lock, closed the outer door, then valved open the inner door.

He stepped into the ship, centered the pistol on the broad back of the man sitting before the instrument board, apparently studying celestial maps.

"Turn around, you," said the man with the pistol.

Thus came Gull Norse.

Lieutenant Marc Sturm turned around as he was bidden. He didn't rise. He turned in the swivel chair slowly, making it plain that he was controlling his terrific surprise. As he turned, he put his elbows back on the board. His left elbow was touching the finger-switch which would shortly activate the force-field.

Gull said as their eyes met, "Sturm, what's your game? I've been following you for eight-nine days. Where you bound?"

His great, red-rimmed, fierce eyes constantly moved over Sturm's calm face. Gull Norse was big. Gull was the shaggy bear of the space lanes. Gull was the big, laughing, life-loving, enigmatic robber whom men hated and loved at the same time. He was the dreadful creature mothers scared their children with. He was a romantic light of glory shining in the imaginary sky of teen-age girls searching for a hero. He was a big lonely brain who murdered the king's English but could at will converse with college professors; and had, some college professors realized later with a start.

He was big, but he had a starvation curiosity bigger than he was. A curiosity that outweighed him, made him top-heavy.

Marc Sturm said, smiling faintly, "Gull, some day your curiosity is going to swallow you in one big gulp, and then there won't be any Gull Norse left."

"Oh, ho! Now what do you mean by that?"

"Well, why did you follow me?"

Gull's ferocious expression changed. He burst into a great thunderous merry laugh. "Listen to him! Why did I follow him! He's crazy! Listen, Sturm. I read the paper, and there it says that that fearless he-man of the Solar Guard is going to bring me in dead. Am I going to let that second lieutenant cavort around space laying some long-range plans to drag me into a net? That second lieutenant is small fry, I say, but even small fry got spitting grease around 'em."

He paused, really laughing, and enjoying his own fanciful verbiage.

"Now I repeat, Sturm: What you got in mind?"

Sturm laughed too. "This," he said. He pushed back with his left elbow. As before, a magnetic stress crackled the air. Through the breakless glass of Gull's helmet, Sturm could see the outlaw's mass of curly black hair part itself in the middle, the hair sticking out horizontal on either side. Then Gull was snapped into the air, his spacesuited legs clicked rigidly together, his arms pressed with invisible clamps to his side. He still held the gun, but was quite powerless to use it.

He rotated slowly, and every time his face came into Sturm's vision it continued to hold hurt surprise.

Finally Gull said accusingly, "Sturm, this is a dirty trick."

Sturm sat down again and leaned back. "I planned it, Gull. Your curiosity was part of the plan. That's a Type-Q force-field, not much different than opposed electromagnets."

Gull's voice was grumpy, "Don't tell me. I know all about a Type-Q field." He blinked a little, then said in a strange tone, a wondering tone, "Yeah, I know all about 'em."

His expression turned cagey. He said in a tone of admiration, "Lieutenant, I never figured you for this much brains. I guess that pilot-blast blow-up was a fancy dodge, all right. Had *me* fooled. But you know, Lieutenant—you know the reason I come here? It was to give myself up."

"Please, Gull," said Sturm. "You pulled a gun on me, remember?"

"Sure I remember. That was just to make you hold still while I told you my story. See, I'm tired of this life. I want to give myself up and get a light sentence and then live like an honest man." His eyes turned humid with moisture. "Have a wife and kids; maybe. I'm not such a bad guy, Sturm. I've never killed a man. I'm just a high-class robber. I can turn back about seventy percent of the loot I've taken in. The other thirty percent I'll work my fingers to the bone to get. I'll show you where the loot is if you'll promise to tell the authorities I give myself up voluntary."

"You would?" Sturm said, his eyes showing his interest.

Gull looked at him doubtfully. "Sure I would. Word of honor." He had a staunch look of honesty in his eyes. When Sturm rubbed at his chin, Gull said, "So how about taking me out of this Type-Q field and declaring a truce?"

Sturm rose, chuckling. He heaved a tremendously long sigh. "Gull, they used to tell me how funny you could be when you wanted to. You're being really funny, now. Nope, sorry. You stay in the field until we get to Mars. I wouldn't take a chance on freeing you. I've got you and I'll keep you—this time."

Gull turned into a raging bundle of straining muscles. The tearful moisture of an honest man disappeared. He hurled some epithets at Sturm and added: "Next time I get a chance I'll strangle you with my bare hands!"

Marc Sturm hit heaven shortly, and roared full blast toward the edge of the boiling zone. Behind him, a disgruntled outlaw had gone sound asleep, hanging helplessly in midair, now and then muttering angrily to himself. The metal parts of his spacesuit were now rigid magnets held in the force-field's locus of energy. In effect, he was a bar magnet, fed from the inductance fields created by the Type-Q magnets in the walls.

Marc Sturm's smile was wry. *Gets-his-man Sturm,* he thought to himself. Still, when the newspapers got this story they'd be bound to temper their write-ups with the respect he deserved. Marc permitted himself to gloat a little. He thought of Colonel Post's grudging reversal of opinion. He thought of Susan's adoration. They made good pictures, good things to dream about. And it was Marc

Sturm's nature to dream—to dream too much. Sometimes about things that hadn't happened yet.

What he didn't dream of was that the dreams might not turn out as planned.

It happened after the ship cut Mercury's orbit, fled at ever-mounting speed through the very fringe of the boiling zone. Marc Sturm rose stiffly from the controls, went through the starboard companionway back to the galley. He made some coffee and cheese sandwiches, with the idea of feeding Gull, but before he could take it out, Gull, apparently wakened by the smell of food, roared through the ship, "Hey, Sturm! I could use some of that coffee!"

It was a good-natured roar, though, and Sturm figured Gull's humor was back. He took a vacuum bottle of the coffee out to Gull, unbuckled his helmet, and held the nipple of the bottle to Gull's lips.

Gull jerked his head back in surprised rage.

"Say," he snarled, "I don't intend to be bottle-fed like any brat of an infant. Why don't you get some gravity aboard this boat?"

"OK," Sturm said genially. He felt he could afford to be genial.

He fired some blasts from a pilot jet. On the vision plate, the celestial panorama—a heavy sheet of stars and one flaming edge of the Sun's corona—began to rotate until it was whirling at a good steady rate. Sturm felt himself gain weight as the centrifugal force created a full Tellurian gravity. He went back to the galley, poured coffee into a cup and brought a cheese sandwich as well.

Gull, of course, was motionless in relation to surrounding space. But he was rotating on an axis in relation to the ship. Sturm, who could walk through the field without danger, as he had carefully excluded items of a metallic nature from his clothing, took hold of Gull's shoulders, made him motionless with respect to the ship. Then, since Gull was still lying exactly on the ship's axis, where there wasn't any gravity at all, he turned him by main force at right angles to his present position.

In this position, Gull was virtually drinking and eating upside down, but there was enough gravity to keep coffee in the cup, and Gull seemed perfectly satisfied with this arrangement. Sturm held him there until he finished eating, then let him go back into the position the force-field demanded.

"That's better," Gull said, smacking his lips. "Don't know why you Solar Guard misters don't like gravity."

"I don't particularly care whether there's gravity or not. Gravity does make eating easier, though."

"Sure it does," Gull said heartily. "Sturm, you're a good guy after all. Why not leave the ship the way she is? No use wasting fuel to rotate the ship every time we eat."

Marc Sturm figured Gull was right. Anyway, it certainly made no difference.

Directly after that, Sturm made a careful checkup of space ahead, saw no sign of dangerous celestial flotsam, put the controls to bed, and went to bed himself, falling instantly asleep.

He as instantly awoke, spine tingling with the most violently horrible sense of catastrophe he'd ever had.

He came tremblingly erect, snatched his flame pistol from the belt hanging on the bunk, went for the control room, panic working on his face. Just then there was a burst of light, showering sparks, the unforgettable odor of pure ozone rushing up his nostrils.

He burst into the control room a second later, was enclosed by that glare. Through the glare, a big hefty figure hurled itself at him.

"Gull!" Sturm yelled incredulously.

Gull was on him, grunting. He caught Sturm's wrist, bent him backward.

"Gotcha now," he shouted amiably.

Sturm went sick all through his body. Kaleidoscopic pictures of horror swamped his brain. Newspaper stories —"the fearless second lieutenant—"; "Uncle Jim—Lieutenant Colonel Susan Quincy outranks you . . . the result of a faulty psychological pattern—"; the psychological portrait with its damning mathematical truths "—general mental capabilities not so good—not so good at all— Rigidity? Yes, very good. Very good indeed. But no brains—no brains—no brains—no brains—"

That all went through his mind. Drops of hot water falling for a thousand years on his tortured head. He went wild, mentally and physically. He broke from Gull's grip, grabbed Gull around the waist and threw him smashingly. The big heavy figure sailed ludicrously through the air. Gull didn't expect anything like that. Nor did Sturm expect Gull to crash into the thousand-and-one fragile parts of the instrument board.

Gull hit the instrument board hard. Glass shattered. The lights went out. The vision plate went gray and blank. The ship leaped like a wild thing, a bucking bronco in midspace. The odor of ammonia from the cooling system was a burning stench. Calcium from the air refiner choked up the air. Lastly the switchboard on the bulkhead shorted itself, made lightning through the ship. In that new glare, Marc Sturm saw the walls of the ship moving backward. Actually, the ship had grabbed him in a mighty fist and tossed him. Tossed him straight forward toward where Gull Norse sprawled. That was the last Marc Sturm knew until he woke up an hour and a half later in a spacesuit.

"I put you in the spacesuit," said Gull Norse amiably. He was hanging onto a guide rail, but the bucking motion of the ship was not intense now. Gull added, " I think that was mighty fine of me. Else you'd have suffocated. But as I say, you're a good guy, Sturm, even if you have got some shortcomings."

"Yeah, I know all about those." Sturm saw he was strapped to the guide rail. He unfastened the strap dully. He looked around the ship. There was one light burning. Too, a quarter section of the vision plate was in operation.

Gull's big flat-planed face was whimsical. "I been working around the ship, getting things shipshape, kind of. Got one light burning, got part of the vision plate operating, found out there's one jet that ain't fused shut. Got the ship on a more or less even keel. Only trouble is, we're inside the boiling zone."

"Inside the boiling zone!"

"Sure. Air in here is hot, like Hades. Our spacesuit thermostats are keeping us cool enough, though. But not for long."

"Not for long?"

"That's it. We're done for." Gull's expression turned genuinely sad, regretful. "I sure hate to cash in my chips now, Sturm. It's a grand life, isn't it? We're falling into the Sun."

"You're sure of that."

"Sure I'm sure. Sturm, remember what I said a while ago about turning myself in and leading an honest life? I almost meant that. Almost. But somehow now that we're about to pass out, I keep thinking of a wife and kids. Sentimental, ain't I?" He was laughing at himself. He stuck his tongue in his cheek and got a thoughtful expression. "Sturm," he said solemnly, "I got a ambition to write poetry."

In spite of himself, Sturm laughed out loud. "You?"

Gull drew himself up, offended. "Mr. Sturm, please be informed that language in all its subtle connotations and nuances strikes a responsive chord in my savage breast. I gain a sheer delight from the work of the old masters— Shelley, Rupert Brooke . . . ah! there was a potential master. Only trouble was he died too young to develop his true capabilities. Then the masters of the light touch— light verse. Gull Norse, for instance. Ah . . . let's see now . . . uh . . . something about . . . Sturm, listen to this:

"Don't trust me, my friends—'twill be your loss
  I'll tell you what's the trouble:
When I make a promise I always come across—
  But mostly double."

Sturm smiled. "A good portrait of the man," he said.

Gull scowled. "I wasn't intending that as a picture of me."

Sturm was impressed. "You made that up on the spur of the moment?"

"Sure I did. Figure what I could do if I had some time. You see, that's the big difference between me and you, Sturm. You figured out a plan to trap me, and I fell into the trap. But it took you a good long time to plan it. You're just too slow to figure things out. Now me, I've got a quick mind. Soon's I got into the trap, I hit on the way to get out. That coffee gag—did you fall for that! You just didn't catch on. See, I'd just as soon suck coffee out of a nipple as the next man, but I made you rotate the ship at a good fast pace in order to simulate gravity so coffee would stay in a cup. I happened to know that I was almost exactly on the ship's axis of rotation. Well, you brought me to a standstill when you gave me the coffee, but remember you couldn't bring ship's air to a standstill. The air kept turning around in the ship. Few hours after you went to sleep, I was spinning around in the ship at a terrific rate, right with the air."

Sturm winced. "Maybe I get it. The metal parts of your spacesuit were cutting lines of force, creating energy strains."

"Sure. The force-field built up to such a high potential there was a power-backlash to the Type-Q force-field machinery. The machinery couldn't take the load. Result, big blow-out and I was free."

A moment later, gloom descended on him. "Lot of good it did," he muttered resentfully.

Marc Sturm stirred from his moveless position. All this while he and Gull had been talking, another part of his mind, a tenacious part, had been working.

He jerked his head at Gull. "You know, Gull, speaking of differences between us, you've already given up. You're ready to stop fighting."

"Oh! Listen to that, would you? He talks about fighting when there's nothing to fight!" Gull made a sarcastic show of talking to a third person.

"You've given up," repeated Sturm, "but I haven't."

Gull looked at him in a very kindly way. "Do we have to starch our upper lips?"

Sturm said simply, "I have to. For one thing, I'm not going to let the Sun incinerate my plans for a promotion and marriage." He hesitated, then smiled. He told Gull about his interview with Post.

Gull looked sympathetic. "Now ain't that a shame when they stuff a man's soul into an equation. You reckon they got a psychological portrait of me too?" he asked with avid interest.

"I should think they would have. They take it pretty early."

"Yeah? How come they ever started a system like that?"

Sturm shrugged dismally. "It's pretty accurate. The Cattell System, they call it, after a twentieth century psychologist."

"Is that so? How d'you suppose I'd stack up under the system, Sturm? I got good brains, for instance."

Sturm nodded. "About .9g, I'd say. And about .4w."

"What's that?"

" 'W' is character integration. Not so good in your case, Gull."

Gull bridled, but Sturm went on, with grim humor. "And about .9c1—that's a Bohemian factor. Say it isn't so! Extraversion? Well, about .8c, I'd say. You're a perfect extrovert, Gull, practically."

Gull grinned broadly. "That makes me out a pretty good guy—except for that 'cl' business. I don't like that. What else?"

"About .4p—rigidity. Which brings us back where I started, come to think of it. Namely, if you're ready to throw in the towel, I'm not. Just a minute."

Sturm left Gull mulling symbols around on his unshaved lips, and hurriedly moved over to the instrument board and extracted a *Star Emphemeris* from a drawer. He opened the paperbound book on the board and leafed through the Bible-paper pages. He spoke with his back to Gull.

"Gull, I happen to remember there's a planet inside the boiling zone about a half million miles. Vulcan. Some scientists landed there eight-nine years ago, but their ships and spacesuits didn't have the insulation value ours have, and the trip was so disagreeable they came back and reported 'nothing of interest.' They did compute the planet's orbit though, degree of libration, diameter, distance from the Sun and so forth.

"It keeps one face to the Sun, but it wobbles sharply back and forth like a perfect pendulum. That creates a 'twilight' zone about a hundred miles wide, where it's hot sometimes, cold others. No atmosphere, but we can land and repair the ship. So maybe—*Hey!*"

He broke into a shout of joy.

Gull came forward, scowling over his shoulder at the *Emphemeris*. His eye caught on the data immediately.

"Well," he rumbled grudgingly, "I guess you got something. Vulcan's less than a hundred thousand miles away!"

Lieutenant Marc Sturm and Gull Norse, the outlaw, landed on Vulcan seven hours later. Only "landed" is hardly an accurate description. The single rocket-jet got them into the fold of the planet's .2 of a Tellurian gravity, and after that it was the planet that engineered the landing.

Up until the very last few moments, Sturm thought that he had done pretty well. But trying to bring a ship into a landing on one jet is similar to trying to balance yourself on the two hind legs of a chair. In this case, the chair tipped.

"We'll have to jump," said Sturm.

Gull Norse already had the air-lock open. They stood on the very lip, watching the whole universe revolve. Sometimes they saw the Sun, one fiery segment of it, anointing the tumbled cliffs and mountains with an hibiscus-scarlet fire; sometimes, as the ship whizzed around like a maddened pinwheel, they saw nothing but clear-cut stars. They finally jumped, when nothing but two hundred feet of vacuum separated them from the planet.

Each held a flame pistol, a small rocket-blast in itself. Each pistol was attached to the waist by a thin chain.

Sturm, tumbling down with a terrific sense of vertigo, saw the scarlet surface rushing up. He shouted, senselessly. He got into position to break his fall with the pistol. He did manage to cushion the collision, as something, a surface that was smooth, shiningly red, somehow liquid, broadened out to receive him. He struck.

Most of his senses were torn away. But he remembered motion, tumbling motion, as if he were in the grip of a sucking current. He was sucked into darkness, rushed along at terrific speed—and then, borne by the same current, went shooting upward at terrific pace.

The upward pace stopped, he seemed to fall back onto something soft and spongy, and he was quiet.

For a while, he thought he must have gone blind. There was no light. His mind worked sluggishly. Under him, his senses told him, there was a spongy, elastic surface. He raised himself by his gauntleted hands, sank up past his forearms. Nothing spongy then; a liquid, buoying him up.

"Gull," he muttered.

No answer. Sturm seemed to hear an oppressive, boxed-in silence. He reached dully into one of the sealed pockets built in one of the sleeves of his spacesuit, extracted a flashlight. He played the beam around. The tiny circle of light made one insignificant hole in the absolute darkness. He was lying on the surface of a pool, though—a pool composed of a heavy, quiet, darkly yellowish substance. But the yellowness was merely the reflection of the beam—he had no way of knowing the true color. But he suspected it would be silver.

It was a roughly circular pool, a body length and a half in diameter. The pale beam picked out cracked, pitted walls which rose in unevenly vertical lines. The flash traveled up ten, twenty, thirty feet, revealed a few narrow ledges. Sturm got an impression of walls narrowing together, but the beam showed only dark obscurity higher up.

Gull Norse was lying rigid a few feet away. Sturm thought to himself, *I've got you, now what do I do with you?*

Gull stirred at that moment, floundered around. Sturm inched toward him by pushing with his hands. He brought Gull to a sitting position. Gull's eyes opened slowly, then narrowed with sharp awareness.

Sturm told what the flash had picked out.

Gull, interest showing in his eyes, said: "A quicksilver pool. I thought we sorta hit something soft. Lucky break."

"I *don't* think we landed in this particular pool," Sturm said. "We were out in the open when we hit. Then I remember moving, as if we were in a current, being sucked along. Looks like we're closed up tighter 'n a drum here. No openings in the walls, near as I can see."

Gull scoffed. "Listen to him. If there aren't any openings in the walls," was his reasoning, "how did we get here? We better take a good look around."

Gull moved around the narrow circle of the walls twice. He was much discouraged. "Nope, not an opening. You're right. Then we came up from beneath."

Sturm hesitated. "From beneath?"

"Sure. Through a fault in the rock."

"Well, maybe. I don't get the picture though. Apparently we hit a quicksilver lake outside, which is connected with this pool. This pool is quiet though. What would cause a current, a flow of quicksilver from the lake to the pool—and a current that's apparently stopped flowing?"

Gull's thick lips worked over each other thoughtfully as he stared at Sturm.

"Hey! Wait a minute—" His tone was startled. He stopped. A quizzical light appeared in his eyes. He stuck his tongue in his cheek, making a bulge. "Naw," he said, "I guess not."

Sturm waited a moment. He said politely, "Any hare-brained idea might lead to something at this point, Gull."

"Naw, it wasn't any good. You know, I think we better scale the heights. Make an ascension, et cetera, and see what goes on up there."

He jerked his helmeted head toward the rising walls. Sturm quietly agreed. He was beginning to distrust Gull again. More, he was distrusting himself. A sentence started going through his mind: *The quick brown fox jumped over the lazy dog. The quick brown fox—*

Gull was quick. And he was foxy. Maybe he was drawing himself up to jump— But how? Yet he had "jumped" out of the Q-type force-field.

They climbed the walls without difficulty, now and then stopping to rest. True enough, the walls continued to narrow. Forty or fifty feet up, Sturm no longer could see the pool. It merged into dark obscurity. Ten feet farther on, they came to a "roof," a smoothly domed continuation of the black basalt walls.

Gull, sitting on a ledge opposite Sturm, looked at Sturm wordlessly. Sturm looked back. Very quietly, he laid the flashlight down, and for several minutes there was no sound. Sturm was bitter. The truth was obvious. He said finally:

"We're bottled up."

"Yeah, I guess so. Bottled up is right. Ever see anything like it? From the fire into the frying pan."

Gull thought that over. "Yeah," he muttered. "Yeah. That's a good thought. From the fire into the frying pan."

Sturm detected something odd about Gull's voice. Gull's teeth were chattering. He suddenly directed the flash on the big man's face. Gull's face was blue with cold. Sturm directed the flash on Gull's hips. He reached across and flipped up a tiny lever.

His voice was sharp. "Didn't you know you were freezing? Your thermostat was off."

Gull grinned. "Aw, I did that on purpose, Sturm. I wanted to see what the climate was in here. Must be below zero. . . . I'll tell you what I've figured so far, Sturm. This bottle we're in is a sort of volcanic bubble. The opening is down under the pool of quicksilver. We couldn't begin to dive under and find the opening—the quicksilver's too thick, weighs too much. So we better forget about getting out from below, and concentrate on blowing out the bottle's cork."

Sturm was vainly trying to read Gull's mind. "Wait a minute," he said sharply. "You wanted to see what the climate was. Why?"

Gull was amiable. "Doubting me? I'll tell you why. There's air in here—volcanic gases that've been trapped in this bottle for a couple million years maybe. The air is cold. That means the walls of this bottle are cold. So what? Why, so we can dig our way out of here with a flame pistol.

"Here's what I mean: As we come floating down from the ship, I seen a lot of rocky hills around here. Low hills, too, maybe sixty or seventy feet. Not higher than this bottle. That means we're pretty close to the top of one of them hills. The rock is cold and if we use the flame pistol the heat'll make it chip off pretty fast. Then we can get out of here. I'll show you."

Gull came to his feet with vigor. He took up his flame pistol, adjusted the valves. A long smoky flame leaped out. Gull adjusted the valves again and it settled down to an inch-thick sword of flaming, violet-blue energy. Gull

152

directed this against the dome of the natural bottle, held it there.

Sturm, watching with interest, felt a solid wave of heat strike him before the refrigerating apparatus in his space-suit took hold. A few minutes later, there was a clean cracking sound. A foot-long slab of rock two or three inches thick cleaved itself away, broke into fragments and fell. Sturm heard them strike the surface of the mercury pool. Gull grinned with triumph.

"See? Why do I have to think of these things?"

Gull, the shaggy bear of the space lanes, was happy. He began to sing as he worked. His voice roared, shook the very walls in their age-old emplacements. He had a re-markable bass baritone. He sang these words:

"Said the man-eating shark to his wife
In their bower so quiet and shady,
Although I am a man-eating shark,
I would not refuse a lady!"

Sturm, sitting with his knees drawn up, laughed. "That yours, too?"

"Naw. That's an oldie. But here's one I made up last year. Soon as you put me in jail where I'll have lots of time, I'll write it up and I'll bet that there magazine *My Stars!* will buy it." Another slab of rock, a little smaller, chipped off. "Listen," said Gull, and recited:

"A Martian wolf saw her whelp chasing
A hunter, and cried, 'Oh, how rude!
Junior, I've told you so often
Never to play with your food!'"

For about two hours, Gull Norse, the fabulous, sang

and recited verses new, old, and of his own creation. Inflexibly he pursued his task. Heat poured from the growing hole in the dome of the bubble. Sturm's refrigerating apparatus was working hard, and to conserve its energy he dropped to a lower ledge. There, completely without intending to, he went sound asleep.

He awoke. The first thing he thought of when he awoke was that Gull Norse had been crooning softly just as he fell asleep. Crooning with a sinister softness, he thought. Maybe Gull *did* have plans to—jump.

He came to his knees wildly, his stomach a cold knot. His relief was indescribable when he looked upward, saw the fierce brilliance of the flame pistol, saw Gull silently working at the growing hole. A few pieces of basalt fell past him as he watched. The tenseness went out of him, he smiled a trifle sheepishly, and worked his way to where Gull was working.

Gull grunted, grinned at him preoccupiedly.

"You been sleeping a couple hours." The cavity was about three and a half feet deep now. "I figure you better go sleep a couple more. We'll work four-hour shifts, eh?"

Several big chunks fell from the aperture. They struck the metal pool below. Gull was holding his head to one side, as if listening to the soft sound as they struck. His manner was oddly tense.

Sturm said slowly, "You know, Gull, I don't think I'd better go to sleep."

"Yeah? Why not?"

"I don't trust you. You might get that hole bored through, crawl out and make your getaway. That's what you've got in mind, isn't it?"

The big man's unshaved face held a wounded expression. "Aw, now. Ain't we in this together? Buddies, pals,

comrades and all that sorta gaff? Besides, where would
I escape to?"

"You'd use the ship to escape in. If we fell in a mercury lake outside, the ship did, too. It's floating out there
and it's probably no worse damaged than it was before
it fell. It'll only take fifteen or twenty minutes at the most
to pry open the fused jet-ends, dummy up some new grid-
connections from the fuel tanks and then take off."

"You think I'd go away and leave you here?"

"I sure do."

Gull's eyes turned humid with unshed tears. He told
Sturm, "When you know nobody in this wide universe
trusts you, Sturm, it makes you feel bad." He sniffed.
"Guess it's my own fault."

Sturm laughed. "Cut the act. Give me that flame pistol
and I'll take over for a while. I don't care what you do.
You go to sleep if you want to, but *I'm* staying awake.
At least you know I won't run off alone—not without
you."

Grumpily, Gull thrust the still-flaming pistol at him,
muttered to himself and let himself down to the next
ledge, and the one below that. Sturm immediately attacked
the cavity, tightened the valve and got still a hotter flame.
Around him, he knew, the atmosphere must be broiling hot.

A few minutes later, he casually looked down the widening walls of the "bottle." He couldn't see Gull.

"Gull," he said sharply, peering down.

"OK," Gull said resignedly. "I'm down here a couple
ledges below the one you was sleeping on. I feel awful
bad, Sturm, and I guess I won't sleep, just thinking about
things. In case I do go to sleep, though, don't you keep
on yelling at me like I was a spoiled brat crossing to the
wrong side of the street."

His voice grew drowsy toward the last. Sturm smiled. Gull didn't realize how much like a spoiled brat he sounded at times.

As has been said, if there was one thing Sturm was good at, it was tenacity. He enjoyed being tenacious. Whether he knew it or not, the theme which governed his life was that contained in the maxim, "A journey of a thousand miles begins with but a single step."

He had very little knowledge, philosophically, of the mechanical advantages given by the lever in the matter of human affairs. Jujitsu would never have appealed to him, for instance, if it had not been a required subject at Decimal Point. Therefore, he was not familiar with the mental jujitsu men of Gull Norse's type use to such great advantage: namely, using the most subtle means of employing others to do their work.

Sturm was now on the long arm of the lever, swinging through a wide, hard arc. While Gull had manipulated himself onto the short arm, where his job was being done for him without using his personal energy.

Not only was Sturm doing Gull's work, he was actually leaving Gull free to pursue a plan which was being brought to completion by Sturm's tenacity.

Sturm didn't know that. It gave him a strange feeling of elation every time the cavity leading to freedom deepened itself by another inch. An inch is only part of a foot. A foot is only part of a mile. Sturm would have been contented to work on the cavity for countless days, if he felt he was getting some place.

He became so absorbed in the job that time, even the situation, lost meaning for him. He worked two hours, three, then four, without once taking the flame from the growing aperture.

Then something struck the wrong note.

The fragments cloven from the solid basalt aperture were not falling and hitting softly. They were not plopping down onto the surface of a mercury pool. They were striking a solid, unyielding substance.

The significance of that false note struck with shattering revelation. He stood motionless, fighting the suffocation that rose in his mind. Then he snapped off the flame, dropped to one knee, whispered hoarsely:

"Gull!"

There was no answer. The name came out sharply the second time. Then Sturm shouted madly with the full power of his throat, "Gull!"

There was not the whisper of an answer, only the lonesome echoes of his own voice. He began to shake with a throttled hatred of himself. His hand shook as he dropped the flame pistol in its holster, began to let himself with a reckless lack of care down the walls of the bottle. He searched every ledge with his flashlight as he descended. When he was three-quarters of the way down, he knew that Gull, the quick brown fox, had jumped over the lazy dog.

Gull Norse was gone.

After a while, moving as if a nightmare had struck with chill abandon, Marc Sturm crept farther down the walls. His flashlight picked up no silvery sheen of placid quicksilver. Where had been the quicksilver pool there was nothing. The quicksilver pool was gone, and the bottom of the pool was a smooth, steeply sloping ledge of basalt leading down to a point on the rim of the bottle.

There was a smooth, circular aperture at the bottom of the slope. Like a tunnel. Gull Norse had crawled through.

How long ago? Sturm had no way of knowing. He had been conscious that something was wrong long before he realized what was bothering him. The deadly stupor in his brain kept him moveless for long minutes as he stared at the cavity. He finally did move, reached the slope, and allowed himself to slide to the cavity.

On hands, on knees, slowly at first, then more quickly, he entered the tunnel. It was apparently a tunnel which would give forth into the mercury lake outside. In his mind's eye, he could see Gull Norse, already at work prying open the jets, getting ready to take off. Suddenly the full meaning of what had happened struck him. He went faster, as fast as his horrified thoughts.

And the unexpected happened.

There was a strange, liquidly articulated sound. The "pop" such as a champagne bottle makes when its cork is removed. Hell broke loose. Lieutenant Marc Sturm did not know what happened—except that he was hurled back along the tunnel, his flashlight torn from his gauntleted hand by an incredible smashing force; that he was lifted at appalling speed, flung with an ear-rupturing howl of violent energies into a maelstrom where thoughts themselves were sheared away, and the mind became silent.

When Marc Sturm's senses came untangled, he saw that the planet Vulcan was below him.

Not only below, but *distant*.

Vulcan was a flat disk the size and color of a copper penny. It completely eclipsed the Sun. Sturm made a few slow computations, using the planet's diameter and its known distance from the Sun as the main factors. From that he figured he was twenty, maybe twenty-five miles above the body. He was out in the vacuum of open space.

The disk of the planet was neither decreasing nor increasing at the moment. That meant he was at that point where he was neither rising nor falling.

Yet, even as he made those deductions, the girth of the tiny trans-Mercurian planet did increase. Gravity had hold of him.

He did not then figure out why he was here, what tremendous force had thrust him explosively into space. He didn't have a chance, for at that moment a new panic laid hold of him. He saw a flash of intense silver some miles out from the planet. Intuitively, he understood what it was.

The spaceship, and Gull in it.

He would have to catch up with it. The thought came to him coldly, incisively, without emotional disturbances. The impossibility of the task did not occur to him. That it would have occurred to most other people in his position he did not realize. But he had to do it, else he would be marooned on a planet which, according to the scientists, held "nothing of interest." Those scientists had been in too much of a hurry to get away from an uncomfortable climate to discover the mercury lake. But their phrase, "nothing of interest," meant at the very least that there was no life, no growing things—no food. The Robinson Crusoe act was out. Therefore he had to reach the ship.

There were certain advantages with him. For one thing, Gull's course was at an acute angle of thirty degrees to his line of fall. Using the reactive powers of the flame pistol, Sturm could cross Gull's trajectory before or when Gull reached that point in space. For another, the flame pistol would not have to bear the full brunt of the load, because gravity would take care of the necessary downward motion. He figured he should meet the ship fifteen miles out from the planet, which meant he had to get closer than he was anyway.

He unholstered the flame pistol, set its aperture to rocket-jet size, and blasted. The first blast made such a difference in his present vertical course that the baleful edge of the Sun peered over a rim of the planet. The second blast put him into the full view of that incredibly malignant furnace. There was no help for it. He pulled the thick blue filter down over his helmet, and steadily gained headway, his overworked refrigerating mechanism issuing its vibrating hum of protest.

Anxiety tore at him the last few moments. He wondered if Gull could see him, or if Gull were using the single vision plate that was still working merely for a forward view. At any rate, Gull had done a hurried repair job on the ship, for it was traveling with the labored toil of an old man walking uphill. It was off-keel. The body of the ship leaned at an angle to the line of flight. Sturm saw that when it was scarcely a mile away.

There was a moment toward the last when Sturm went frantic, knowing he would overshoot the mark. There was another moment, as the patrol ship came rushing along, that he knew it would breeze on past him. But there was the moment that counted, as he fired countless panicky bursts from the flame pistol, when he knew he was going to strike the target as squarely as was necessary—and seconds later did strike it.

He hit broadside on. He struck with such force that he couldn't see how Gull could help but have heard him. He grabbed at a stubby, projecting periscopic eye, hung on through a daze of pain and smashingly emptied lungs. But he was here.

It had taken him forty minutes. He knew that another ten or fifteen minutes would have been fatal, for his refrigerator was working at a task it had not been designed to perform. It was about to burn out. Minutes later, the solid phalanxes of heat marching in such violent profusion from the tongued Sun would have boiled the blood in his veins.

There was still danger of that. He therefore crept along the flanks of the ship, inched down over the bulge of the nose, taking care not to get caught in the eyepiece of the two periscopic eyes whose lenses weren't shattered. He was in shadow now. He lay there, relieved, yet he knew that a nerve-shattering vigil lay ahead of him.

At this velocity, it would take the ship twenty or thirty hours to get out of the boiling zone. Sturm had to wait until then before he put his plan in motion. Even then, the Sun's heat would be a mighty, destroying thing, and he would be able to work only a half hour at a time. But the job had to be done. Meanwhile, he must wait.

It was forty hours before the ship left the rim of the boiling zone. Marc Sturm felt like a mere husk of a man. He had chained himself to a grab rail, he had slept a few hours, he had sucked water from a tube in his suit, but he hadn't eaten. In a full gravity, he would not have been able to move. But he did.

He again crawled into the full glare of the Sun, to the very stern of the ship, where he again used his flame pistol. He was attacking the jets. He was going to fuse them right back up again.

He worked for thirty minutes at a time. His refrigerator was already deficient, for at the end of that time sweat began to form. He would then crawl back into the shadow again.

He kept this up for interminable hours—crawling sternward, then abaft, sternward and abaft.

It took him three hours to close one jet out of the six that were working. His process was simple but awkward and difficult. He played a white-hot flame on the stubby ends of the jets until they glowed with a violet intensity that would have crisped flesh in seconds. Then he put the metal heel of his space boot on them and pressed. Several such operations soon squeezed the lips together. The pointed streamers of flame erupting from the jets would thin out to nothing.

It took him a little over twelve hours to render four jets useless. During that time, a stupefying hunger wrenched his vitals, a terrible exhaustion threatened to destroy his volition toward movement. Each movement, in fact, seemed to come from his will rather than his body.

In the intervals when he was in shadow, he lay on his back, staring with burning, red-rimmed eyes at the stars. His hands were wrapped around guide rails with the grip of death. He thought he might be a little delirious when he saw the stars subtly change pattern—and there were the constellations of Lieutenant Colonel Susan Quincy; of Uncle Jim Post; of Gull Norse, the fabulous. There was a clear-cut psychological portrait written right on the skies, and sometimes it told him he didn't have any brains. Then in the same breath it would say, "But, Buddy, you sure got guts."

That made him feel better, and he would start crawling back to the job, though the various things in his body were telling him he was a little bit crazy in the head for thinking he could move at all. But he finished the job—four jets— and went back to his resting place.

He slept. In his sleep he saw Gull, so terribly unhappy when he saw his jets blanking out one by one. Gull Norse had only two jets. He had just enough power to get to the little errant asteroid where Sturm had, days before, arranged a crash landing. That's where he was going, so he could repair the ship again. Sturm went more soundly toward sleep, remembering with a dutiful sigh that he had strapped himself to the grab rail; but not remembering why he had fused the jets.

There was a jar which shook Sturm awake. His eyes snapped open. He fought to bring his thoughts back to normal. The little links of the chain of memory fell into place, and he had the story. Not only the story, but revived strength. He was abruptly frantic. He turned over to hands and knees, unstrapped himself, got unsteadily to his feet.

The ship had landed. And true enough, it had landed on the little asteroid.

Panting, almost retching with weakness, Sturm urged himself across the top of the ship in a weaving stagger. He got amidships just in time to look over the edge and see the air-lock opening. Gull Norse's big spacesuited body came out. Marc Sturm jumped without a second's fore-thought. He landed on Gull's shoulders. With the same motion, he brought the butt end of the fifteen-pound flame pistol down on that part of Gull's spacesuit where it touches the back of the head. He brought it down with every ounce of strength he had. It hit solidly. Gull Norse didn't utter a sound. He crumpled up. He fell straight down on his face, arms loose strings draped on the ground, legs tangled up like those of a dead man.

And Sturm fell beside him.

Again he knew he must move, though. He did. He went into the ship, rifled the lazaret amidships, found some coils of rope, and made thirty different turns around Gull's body, starting at the ankles, before he tied a Gordian knot. When Gull woke up three hours later, Lieutenant Marc Sturm had drunk three cups of coffee, some soup, had pried open the jets again, and the ship was on the way to Mercury, seven hundred thousand miles distant.

Gull's eyes were tiny slits.

"What you think this is, Sturm, a second-rate tele-audio program, tying me up like this?"

Sturm's smile was wry. "I guess my methods entail sheer

brute force rather than brains, Gull. Anyway, you stay tied up until we get to Mars. We're on the way to the Mercurian garrison to get a new ship first, though. Now, while we've got some time, why don't we talk about that bottle? How you tricked me, for instance— I've told you how I tricked you."

"I'll say you have," Gull muttered. His head turned continuously back and forth, giving the impression of a leopard pacing a cage.

He was unable to move more than a few muscles. In addition to the profusion of ropes, chains bound him full-length to the deck plates.

Gull muttered, "Wasn't anything to it. Just a matter of atmospheric pressure in the bottle, of the planet's libration, of the Sun's heat. That mercury lake was right in the middle of Vulcan's twilight zone. Every fifteen or twenty hours the planet made a complete wobble. That meant for half of that time the lake was right out in the full glare of the Sun—first moving out and then moving back. The other half of the wobble it moved through the cold zone. There were two extremes of heat.

"You can figure what happened when a few thousand degrees of heat poured straight down on the lake. It heated up fast. It transmitted its own heat to the atmosphere in the bottle. The atmosphere in the bottle expanded just as fast, pushed the mercury pool back into the lake outside. Not far enough to lose its atmosphere, though.

"We fell into the lake just as it moved back into the cold zone. Y'know, when superheated air cools, it cools fast, like that. It contracted with a bang. It sucked mercury right back up into the bottle, and we were sucked up with it. Remember I tested the temperature of the atmosphere in the bottle. It was cold. So I figured I was right."

Gull stopped, scowling. His good nature was gone. "I guess you really got me this time, Lieutenant."

"I guess so."

"Well, then figure it out yourself."

Sturm said ruefully, "I guess it's all figured out—except a few things. I suppose Vulcan's lack of atmosphere helped. No diffusion of heat. When the lake got into the Sun's rays, there must have been several thousand degrees of unadulterated heat pouring on it. Probably the lake came near close to boiling, all the way through. When it got in the cold zone its temperature changed to the other extreme —maybe got close to absolute zero.

"Come to think of it, the lake would evaporate after a while, wouldn't it, Gull?" Sturm rubbed his chin. "Maybe it's fed from an underground well. Maybe."

He sat there puzzling it out. The jigsaw took shape.

"I guess I was a dope, Gull—running true to character. You used me by making up a tall story about a 'cork' we could chip out with a flame pistol. The only reason you wanted the flame pistol working was to superheat the volcanic gases in the bottle—same as if the mercury lake were in the Sun. The gases expanded, pushed the quicksilver pool back into the lake outside. You crawled through the tunnel, found what was left of the pool, forced yourself under a few feet by using your flame pistol, then went shooting up to the surface. And all the while, I was heating up the air so you could make your getaway.

"In a way, that setup was vaguely similar to a big thermometer or barometer. Bet you could duplicate it in a laboratory, eh? Or on a stove, maybe. Put an open mouth jar mouth-down in a shallow pan of water. Boil well. Turn off heat. Hm-m-m." He stopped.

After a while, Gull grinned in sickly fashion. "You sure were a sucker," he said. "Only thing is, like the papers say, you always get your man. Guess I gotta respect you. Tell your chief for me."

"I'll do that."

"Tell him . . . say, listen, Sturm, tell him I wasn't intending to leave you back there. I was gonna radio SAG and tell 'em where you were. I was gonna tell 'em that, honest to God.

"Of course, how was I to know that 'cork' was actually there and the gas-pressure would blow it off and send you shooting up into space like a cannon ball? But my intentions were good. You believe me, Sturm?"

Sturm said, "I think I do believe that, Gull."

Gull's face wreathed with flamboyant smiles.

"Sturm, that makes me feel mighty good. You're one of the best guys in this here solar system, don't forget it. And you know what I'm gonna do soon as I get in jail? Sturm, I'm gonna lay plans to lead a honest life hereafter. I'm gonna plan to become a great humanitarian—help the sick and needy, the halt and the lame, and all that sorta gaff. And in my spare time, I'm gonna write poetry. Sturm, I'm gonna become one of the champeen light-verse writers of all time!"

Two days after Marc Sturm deposited Gull Norse at the Fontanaland detention barracks, and received a receipt acknowledging his safe delivery, he stepped from the elevator in Satterfield Hotel on his way to report to Uncle Jim Post. When he handed his key in the clerk at the desk gave him an ethergram, saying:

"Lieutenant—" He caught himself, his eyes widening as he saw the five glittering, star-studded stripes on Sturm's right shoulder.

"Pardon me—I mean captain. Captain Sturm, the Interspace Radio Company people asked me to inform you that this ethergram was sent from an unidentified space-ship which had left Fontanaland a few hours before."

Sturm felt a chill presentiment. With stiff fingers, he tore the envelope, fumbled open a pink slip. The ether-gram was unsigned. It was a four-line jingle. It read:

As you and the leopard are opposite types,
    I leave you with these thoughts:
Riddle, riddle, you've changed your stripes,
    Can the leopard change his spots?

Fifteen minutes later, absolutely wooden-faced, Sturm stepped into the presence of Colonel Post.

Post was obviously controlling himself only by a moun-tainous effort. He said chillingly, "Captain, allow me to congratulate you on a brilliant piece of work. Since our last conversation, you've given me ample reason to be proud of you."

"There was nothing brilliant about it, sir. As I've ex-plained to you, I'm afraid I don't major in brilliance."

Post made a grinding noise of rage with his teeth. "I could name a few other people—namely, the commanding officer at the Fontanaland barracks—who don't major in brilliance either; or anything else. Captain Sturm, I have another assignment to hand you. *Now*."

"Yes, sir?" Sturm lifted a dark eyebrow.

"Captain Sturm, this morning Gull Norse escaped Fon-tanaland."

"Yes, sir?"

"Your work has gone for nothing. Therefore, I'm set-ting you on Norse's trail again."

"No, sir."

Post stiffened. "What d'you mean, 'no, sir'?" he snarled.

"I differ with you, sir. My work hasn't gone for nothing.

I've received a deserved promotion. Also, according to the rules and regulations of the SAG, sir, as I have just finished an assignment, I am permitted to take time off for a honeymoon if I so desire."

"A honeymoon? Why, confound it, don't you go springing rules and regulations on me. According to the rules, I can postpone your marriage if there's urgent business to be attended to— Ah, so you've seen Susan?"

Sturm smiled slightly. "I saw her yesterday afternoon —when we were married."

Post groaned, groped to a seat and breathed hard for a moment. "Congratulations, Captain," he muttered. "And offer my best wishes to the bride. But what are we going to do with Gull? *What are we going to do with that man?*"

"I think, sir," said Sturm politely, "that he must have been reading too much poetry lately. Namely, the one that begins, 'Stone walls do not a prison make, Nor iron bars a cage—' "

Jafee, my "dummy" president, was boiling. He called me by radiophone as soon as he got in from Venus.

"You can't keep this up," yelled Jafee. "D'you want a revolution on your hands?"

"We won't have a revolution."

"I'm the guy that takes the brunt of all this," he yelled. "There's a hundred thousand Venusians on my hands and they're screaming bloody murder. They're yelling worse than I am. They want better working conditions. They want normal Earth pressure. They want better wages. They want heat. The mines get cold!"

"I can't do anything about it," I insisted.

"They'll get you!" he hissed.

"Aw, be yourself, Jafee. Nobody even knows I own

Venusian Metals. And even if they did, they couldn't prove it. You tell them if they don't like the way things are, they better ship back to Earth where they came from. And another thing. Maybe you won't like this. But another wage cut goes into effect June first."

He was shocked into silence. Then he broke down. "Chief," he said wearily, "I suppose you must be runnin' into financial difficulties. I suppose you have to treat these fellows the way you do to make your profit. But I'm tellin' you it's better to lose money than trample human beings the way you're doing."

"I can't help it," I snapped. "It's the way the system is run. I abide by the rules of the game."

"I guess so," he said wearily.

Before I hung up, I cautioned him once more never to mention my name in connection with Venusian Metals, and he agreed listlessly. Jafee was chickenhearted. I couldn't be—not if I wanted to make a nice showing on my books.

That night I was eating alone, at the Sky Garden. Music was playing, and the moon was shining.

I had just finished my aperitif, and was studying the menu, when a short, somewhat plump man with a scar across his clean-shaven face weaved his way round the dance floor and seated himself at my table.

"D'you mind if I sit here?"

"There's other tables," I pointed out significantly.

Then I met his eyes, and my skin chilled.

"Perhaps I shouldn't have asked you," he said in his soft voice. "Perhaps I should say that I sat here with the single intention of telling you a story."

"A story?" I managed huskily.

"Yes." He laughed genially, and, as the waiter came up, took it upon himself to wave the waiter away. The waiter went away and I said nothing.

"First," he resumed, "the story concerns six men, of whom there now remains but one. Also, it concerns a planet where you can make a jump of one hundred nineteen miles, in a straight line, and land on the same planet."

My throat was dry. I remembered Venusian Metals, which I owned. I had the impression of a cat playing with a mouse.

"This story has a moral," he went on. There was mockery behind his genial blue eyes. "A moral which I hope you have no trouble finding. Let us begin."

And he ordered himself a highball and began.

His voice flowed evenly; his voice painted pictures. As he spoke, the music, and the gaily laughing couples, and the moon of the Sky Garden faded away. The word pictures he painted so artistically, combined with my own imagination, carried me back ten years. The story began to unfold in a secluded, richly furnished room atop the Venus Building. Men were there, big business tycoons, huddled around a table; six of them.

John March—owner of freight lines, airlines, trucking concerns—was speaking, his too-steady, slightly distended eyes roving around to meet those of his audience.

"We could control the world market," his pompous voice rumbled. "I tell you, it's as good as done, if we get together on the idea!" He leveled a thick, rigid forefinger at each of them in turn. "Hagerstown, food distributor throughout the Western Hemisphere. Probably the most powerful of us all. Latham, food distributor throughout Asia, Europe, and parts of Australia. Wright, food retailer in I don't know how many countries; but he's managed to sneak his companies in so that he has a fine network across the world. Lemley, chain-store owner if there ever was one. Myself"—he tapped his swelling chest pompously—"transportation: railroad freight lines, airlines, and trucking concerns. Vane, shipper: he could keep wheat and a dozen other staple products out of Europe with his signature alone.

"What does all this lead up to? Listen!" And they listened, and they watched, March's own enthusiasm striking fire to their own; filling their minds with plans; unfolding a picture that was worth looking at!

They saw March's immense, ringed hands trace the picture of a narrow-necked bottle. The lower part of the bottle, said March significantly, represented the food supply; represented the farmers, and the billions of acres of food-producing land.

"Seal off the neck of the bottle!" said March, his distended eyes glowing. "How do you get the stuff inside *out*? How?

"You don't," said March. He hunched forward, whispering. "Gentlemen, we are the neck of that bottle! The outlet! The food distributors, the retailers, the transporters. Need I go on?"

Hagerstown, the food distributor of the Western Hemisphere, coughed delicately. He was a thin, emaciated sort of man. "It sounds foolproof," he admitted cautiously. "Then the idea is to broaden our holdings, squeeze out the independents—"

"—and jack up prices," the chain-store owner Lemley put in, snapping his thin fingers. "It's a cinch, if there ever was one!"

Latham—the food distributor—drummed an expensive eversharp on the glassed-over table, his expressionless, slightly ironic face turned toward Hagerstown. "Yes," he agreed, "it's a sound idea. I, for one, make no objections.

But it means that we have to strengthen our own forces by combining." He smiled with a trace of derision. "We'll keep it secret. And in order to protect ourselves—I don't think any of us would mind sticking knives in the others' backs—we'll sign certain agreements. Count me in, March."

"Me, too," said Lemley.

Vane and Wright added their votes, and lastly, in accordance with his overcautious principles, Hagerstown came in.

There was wine, and it made a pleasantly gurgling sound as it was poured.

March stood up, rocking back and forth on his heels, a pleased, pround expression on his heavy face.

"Gentlemen, to the food monopoly!"

Six glasses clinked, and the toast was drunk.

They spent a few minutes justifying themselves.

"What's dirty about it?" said Lemley. "It's the system we live under, understand? It's dog eat dog! Now, fellows, it looks to me like the first step lays with Vane. We'll starve England—gently, of course." He went on talking, and Andreas Vane listened, at times interspersing florid, genial comments, his whole body shaking as he laughed.

They discussed, these six men, and the more they discussed it, the more plausible and honest it became. They glowed with their own enthusiasm. What couldn't be done with the food monopoly? Food ruled man!

During a momentary silence came an interruption.

The walls, which, as is the common belief, have ears, broke loose from their age-old silence and spoke.

"A commendable plan," said the walls. "Will you remain motionless, while I decide which of you is the filthiest?"

And they remained motionless, for the voice of the walls held a threat that congealed their blood and stiffened

172

their muscles so that they quickly became statues acquiring a green patina.

The calm, derisive voice of the walls said: "You first, Derek Lemley. I think very little of you. You've done so many dirty things I can't begin to remember them all. You've treated the human race like the devil. Your chain stores are a sore on the planet. Most of your products are stamped with the seal of approval of the Housewives Food Purity League—a seal of high value in the minds of all people, including yourself; since it is your own, concealed, self-operated invention.

"Andreas Vane," said the voice of the walls, without a second's hesitation, "your name is appropriate. You are proud and vain and fat, and eternally boasting your selfmadeness; rose from the gutter; devoted every minute to getting ahead. As I recall it, you used to curse the capitalist for holding you down; now you're a capitalist and holding others down—

"Hagerstown, you are unspeakable. A cautious, timid soul of a man, you like to stick daggers in your opponents' backs. Thus you have won out; by making sure there was no opposition; that nothing could strike out at you.

"March, John March. A man as men go, though there are unhealthy blue lines under his eyes, and his overfed stomach is beginning to protrude. A rascally scoundrel, who has taken by brute force, beaten his opponents down with one thought: to rise above them and secure the power he needs to feed his vast ego.

"Robert Latham, I confess that I like you, at times. You see yourself for what you are. You can sneer at yourself. You can see through the petty artifices of others. Thus, you are tolerant, though impatiently so. You can be strong at times, but your own self-condemnation weakens you. But this does not excuse you from your just deserts. You are greedy, you are a trampler. You used to have a splendid body, but excesses are beginning to decay it. So much for you.

"Henry Wright, your hypocrisy is too obvious! Studying your face now, I would feel a burst of doubt if I did not know you well. You look much younger than your thirty-nine years; perhaps in your early twenties; just a young, inexperienced little man, caught in the net set by five others, eh? Is that what your china-blue eyes and your innocent expression is supposed to mean? I'm sorry. Try your hypocrisy on others; it will work, as it has in the past.

"That completes the roll."

The Voice was silent.

March's thick lips set.

"Who are you?" he said, without moving.

"It doesn't matter."

"How d'you know so much about us?"

"Made it my business. I supposed that some day I'd have to judge you."

March's temper was beginning to rise.

"You judge us!" he snarled. "I'll teach you to judge!" His chair clattered back. He came to his feet, angry red lights flickering in his eyes. He started toward the wall closet, for it was there his realistic mind knew the intruder was. He started—and that was all. Something touched his sleeve, lightly. He looked down. The sleeve of his coat was singed, badly, and one side of the cuff was gone.

Nobody had seen from which direction the flash had come.

March stood frozen.

Lemley's thin lips moved. "Better show your good sense," he muttered.

Breathing heavily, March slowly returned, picked up his chair, and sat down.

The Voice said mockingly, "Resistance is useless, I assure you.

"I have, as you may guess, a little plan. The question is, I think, whether any of you is fitted to survive. You may remember the law of survival of the fittest? It has gone quite to pot since the Industrial Revolution. Perhaps it can be revived for a short time. I wonder which of you is most fitted for survival.

"And, not only do I wonder, but I am going to make the experiment. It should be enjoyable. A game. Something to amuse me. To avenge the world at the same time. Yes, it shall be done. Please remain motionless."

And there was a flash of light before their eyes.

Andreas Vane cowered back from it, knew it for what it was, in his last moment of consciousness. An anesthetic bomb. A sickening odor that could take all semblance of life from a man's body. Andreas Vane was a quick thinker, in spite of his smugness. He tried to hold his breath. No use. He had the momentary gratification of knowing that the others had been caught, too. Everything was dark, then.

Vaguely, after that, he felt the rumbling vibration of a ship cutting through the emptiness. His hardening arteries almost burst with outraged pride. He almost woke. But again came the sickening odor.

The next time he awoke, he struggled out of his torpid state without hindrance. He came to full consciousness cautiously. Quiet, all around; and though he strained his ears, he heard nothing. His eyes were still closed; he felt his muscles balling, his nerves beginning to stretch.

He forced himself to remain calm, and did.

He opened his eyes and saw light. Light? It was so dim that it was just about two shades above darkness. It was a pale-violet in color, ghostly, and came from the sides and below. He made the astounding discovery that he was standing—which was not astounding at that, since he felt, instinctively, that there was no gravity. He wriggled his corpulent fingers and discovered they were incased in gloves. Gloves of a pliable, thin material; the kind they used with spacesuits. Nonconductors. That one fact gave Andreas Vane part of the picture, and his pendulous lips began to tremble. He clamped them determinedly.

He was quite evidently clad in a spacesuit, and breathing air from a tank, and being kept warm with electric coils. He moved his arms, discovered the niche in the side of his suit from which these operations were controlled. Besides them there were other buttons and tiny, finger-sized switches.

His flesh crawled. "The experiment begins," he said to himself huskily.

Gingerly, he tried to raise one foot. He failed. He stooped over, and looked at his feet. His shoes—if shoes they could be called—were large, massive, metallic. The surface they were resting on was metallic. His shoes, quite evidently, were magnetic, and were the only thing that held him in one spot.

The light, he saw, came from no one direction. It simply emanated. He decided that the metallic surface—for it was that—was fluorescent, or something akin to that. The surface itself was wavy, had no projections, no rubble, and stretched away to all sides until he failed to see it anymore.

The peculiar thing was that he seemed to be at the bottom of a huge bowl, for the metallic land stretched away and lost itself to his eyes at a distance which must have been five or ten miles at least.

He discovered, suddenly, that he could move, by sliding his magnetic shoes across the metallic surface. Moreover, he found a switch which regulated the current flowing into the shoes. He essayed a few steps.

"Must be an asteroid," he muttered. His bushy eyebrows drew down in a frown. In the half light, he made more discoveries. One was that strapped around his waist, hanging from his right side, was a plain scabbard; in the scabbard was a sword. Vane drew it halfway, shuddering. It was a long, slim, horrible-looking weapon; it fluoresced in the violet light, a slim needle of death.

His jowls quivered. "Ugh!" With repulsion, he started to throw it away; but suddenly remembered the Voice, and thus retained his grip. He returned the weapon to its scabbard, shivering. Where were Hagerstown, Lemley, March, Wright, and Latham? Near here, somewhere?

Other articles he found were: a powerful flashlight, a food kit, swung across his back; a pair of powerful binoculars, and—an ordinary, old-fashioned six-shooter in a holster on his left hip.

Lastly, he discovered that his helmet was equipped with a radio sending and receiving outfit. He expelled his breath in relief. This was more like it!

Every operation was controlled by switches and buttons set into the niche at the hip of his suit. With an eager, jerky motion, he snapped the headset on.

He wet his lips. Then, "Halloo! Halloo! March! Lemley! You, Hagerstown! Halloo, there!"

His flaccid lips were beginning to set disappointedly when a carrier wave abruptly sounded. A voice—the Voice, Vane knew it was—spoke.

"Very good, Vane! You have collected your wits more swiftly than the others. I would advise you, incidentally, to retain all your equipment. Particularly—if I may suggest it—your sword."

The Voice would not speak again, no matter how pleadingly Vane addressed, nor how badly he lost his considerable temper.

He shouted and yelled, but only succeeded in deafening himself. His lips curled bitterly and he was silent. He looked at his right hip resentfully, and shivered.

Why did he need the sword?

He walked around for a while, his sweating face strained. Then he stopped, and devoted himself to getting in touch with his associates. He kept his receiver on constantly, until he had the good sense to conserve power. Thereafter, he turned it on at intervals of two minutes.

March came in on a flood of invective, and Vane, wincing, shut off the receiver for a few seconds until the tirade stopped. During that time, Hagerstown came in, frightened, bewildered, pleading.

Lemley's voice, thin, irritated, snapped back at him. "Oh, for God's sake, shut up! Who all's on the line?"

"Latham and Wright are missing, so far," Vane said. "They'll come in. Where are you?"

"Don't be silly!" snarled March. "Where're *you?*"

Hagerstown's thin, frightened voice started to speak, but Latham, coming in with a burst, drowned him out; and Wright's soft, resentful voice came after his. For a while, Vane's helmet was a madhouse, with five different, metallic voices blasting away at the same time.

"Damnation!" he bawled angrily, thus getting into it himself. But it remained for March's bull voice to shock the others into silence.

"Shut *up!*" he roared. "Who's got any ideas? Shut *up!* You, Hagerstown!"

Hagerstown, the food distributor, said in a strained voice: "I'm not certain. The gravity's so weak, we must be on an asteroid."

"What d'you mean—weak?" Wright said. "There isn't any at all."

"Where're the stars?" Lemley demanded of Hagerstown, witheringly.

Latham spoke up, his well-bred voice faintly amused. "Outside, of course. The whole thing's too obvious. Our friend dropped us into a hole in the ground."

March growled reluctantly, "I guess Latham has got it right. By the way." He tried to keep the gruff note in his voice, but failed. "Who else has a—sword?"

Apparently, everybody, not only had a sword, but a Colt revolver, binoculars, flashlight, and food kit, in addition to the regular appurtenances of a spacesuit.

"Something," said Lemley cheerfully, "is very, very screwy."

"We've been kidnapped," March rumbled dangerously.

Wright smirked, "That's news."

Hagerstown's teeth made a rattling sound. "It . . . it's a plot. Some rival concern, out after our interests."

"It's that damned . . . that damned Voice," said March tensely, a raw note of fury creeping into his tone. "I'm going to see personally, that he gets what's coming to him, the bloated, egotistic—"

"*S-sh!*" Hagerstown's voice blasted out in a scared whisper. "How d'you know he's not listening to us? No sense aggravating the man! Treat him softly!"

"To hell with that!" Lemley snapped contemptuously. "Treat him the way he deserves. If you—"

"How about listening to me for a second?" Vane bit out angrily. "Of course the Voice is listening to us. He spoke to me," Vane said self-importantly. He added significantly: "He told me to be sure and keep my sword."

March explosively started to speak, and suddenly subsided, in shock. There was a strained silence. "Wh-what's the reason for that?" Hagerstown stammered. "Swords? Dangerous beasts down here?"

"Dangerous beasts? Yes, indeed! They are called: March, Vane, Lemley, Hagerstown, Wright, and Latham!

"Each of you will need his sword and his revolver and his wits to protect himself against the other beasts. Do you understand?

"Who said that?" March broke the silence.

"I didn't," said Vane. His nerves were thrumming, and the palms of his hands were more clammy than was ordinary.

Other denials floated in like ghostly whispers.

"It was the Voice," whispered Wright. "I guess he's having his little joke." He laughed hollowly.

Lemley made an irritated sound. "All right, Voice," he snapped. "What d'you mean? What's the joke, then? What fool trick you trying to pull on us?"

"No joke and no trick, I assure you," said the Voice amusedly. "You may consider yourselves beasts in an arena, each fighting the others to the death. A free-for-all, you know. Each trying to win out over the others. And one—and only one—winning out.

"Each," said the Voice, mockingly, "trying to corner the food supply."

March's breath broke loose. "You're talking out of your head."

"I am telling you that one of you beasts will, at the end of—five weeks, shall we say?—yes, at the end of five weeks, one will remain alive. Simply because he possesses the food monopoly. What is so wrong with that? There is no food on this world, save what you now possess yourselves, in your food kits. Why is that different than cornering the food supply on another world, the Earth?

"It is the same, of course," the Voice went on smoothly.

"Each of you has enough food in his kit to last him three days; and water enough for three days. By being charitable, I would suggest that each of you can live, on what he now has, about five days. But what if *one* man should manage to get *all* the food available? The food and water that the others have? I should think he could keep himself alive for five weeks at least." The Voice hovered liltingly. "It all works out very cleverly, you see."

"You're seriously contemplating this?" said Latham, in a voice that had turned to steel.

"*I'm* not contemplating it. *You* are. I simply set myself up as a judge, lay down the rules, and reward the winner with what I conceive to be a just reward—freedom. He who lusts most for survival will, I believe, be the lucky man."

"What if we decide not to play the game?" That was March, snarling.

The Voice was almost sorrowful. "I think," it said, "that you will."

"*I* won't!" Hagerstown quivered. "I'd never enter into anything like that. March! Latham! Vane! Y-you wouldn't, I know!"

"Why," said the Voice, "did you omit Lemley and Wright?"

There was a moment of shocked silence. Hagerstown whispered, in a voice that made Vane's scalp tingle, "You wouldn't—would you, Lemley?"

Lemley chuckled. "Pick your own hearse, lanky!"

"Shut up, Lemley!" March roared furiously. "And you, Hagerstown, don't be such a sniveler. That's Lemley's idea of a joke."

"*Ha-ha!*" said Lemley in faintly disgusted tones.

"Of course," resumed the Voice, still mockingly, "it may come about—by a very long chance indeed—that you'll all band together and refuse to treat each other as beasts of the arena. In which case, of course, you'll all starve together."

Wright said plaintively, in his young voice, "I don't see what *I've* done to merit this. It's unfair. Besides"— he hesitated—"even if we wanted to get together, we couldn't. There isn't any way to locate each other."

The Voice chuckled. "Sure you just want to get together, Wright? Maybe— Well, let that go. About locating each other, it's very simple. Each of you, perhaps you've noticed, has a different carrier wave tone. You'll doubtless learn which carrier wave belongs to which person. By rotating the loop antenna atop your helmets so that the carrier wave you want comes in at its strongest —that is, by taking the minimum—you'll be able to locate the person you want to locate. In order to find out which direction the tone is coming from, you'll find four collapsible iron grids which, when expanded, will cut off radio waves from any direction you choose. By a process of elimination, then, locating one another is quite simple; be he friend or—victim."

"Victim!" gasped Hagerstown rackingly. "You . . . you fiend! You expect us to hunt each other out, for the mere purpose of continuing to live? We won't, you understand? I know what we'll do," said Hagerstown, with a sudden burst of inspiration. "We'll band together. We can hear your carrier wave, too. We'll hunt you out, and butcher you the way you want us to butcher each other."

"No, Hagerstown," said the Voice, with pity. "I think that nothing like that will happen. For, you see, I am outside the planet, you are inside. And there is no way out —for you. Come, come!" the Voice said coaxingly. "Don't you see there's no alternative? Give yourselves up to this game, for the longer you delay, the less becomes the food supply, and, therefore, the greater the demand. If you delay too long, it is likely you'll be forced to resort to—cannibalism."

"My God!" said Hagerstown, and sounded as if he were going all to pieces.

"Ugh!" said Lemley. "I've heard that no matter how you fix human steaks, they still turn your stomach."

"Your sense of humor is cutting," snapped Latham in disgust. "Listen you, whoever you are, I have no intention —at the present time, anyway—of killing anybody. But you forgot ammunition belts for these out-of-date Colts."

"The guns are loaded," said the Voice. "That will be sufficient. There are a few other points I will have to mention. One of them is that you can jump."

"Jump?" said Vane, the shipper.

"Wherever you want to. Perhaps you've suspected that the arena in question is a hollow planet, quite perfectly hollow, too. A few feet more than one hundred nineteen miles, I believe. You see?"

"Ye gods, no!" Vane said in exasperation. "How could we jump anywhere we wanted to? We'd simply fall back."

"Of course you would—if there were any gravity to pull you down. But there isn't any in a hollow planet. You can, therefore, jump clear across the diameter, one hundred nineteen miles, and you'll land at exactly the speed you take off. I advise you, by the way, to land on your feet; and the second you land, you activate the electromagnet in your shoes. The interior of the planet is entirely metallic.

"A few other points: The planet has a rotational period of twenty-five hours plus. All six of you are on the equatorial line, spaced evenly. The lineup is as follows: Latham,

Lemley, March, Wright, Vane, Hagerstown. The planet rotates in that direction; from Latham to Lemley, and so on.

"I think," mused the Voice, "that that is all. Now, I need only to watch. Good hunting, my friends. And, rest assured, I'll return in five weeks. Good-bye!"

"Wait a minute!" Hagerstown screamed piercingly.

But the Voice was gone, and its carrier wave with it.

"Do something, you fools!" shrieked the food distributor. "Can't you see what this means?"

"Shut up, Hagerstown!" said Latham, in a cold voice. There was a long, uncomfortable silence.

Latham spoke again, coldly. "There has to be some kind of organization here. I would advise each of you to take the minimum on everybody else, and try to keep everybody's location in mind. Then, if anybody starts roaming, we'll gang up on him."

Lemley snickered. "You forget we can't keep our waves on all the time. Fact is, if we were smart, we'd shut them off whenever possible. We have to conserve power."

"Shut up for a minute and give us a chance to get your location," said Wright sullenly. "I'm not taking any chances."

"You don't have to be afraid of me," babbled Hagerstown. "I'm telling you right now I'm not—"

"You make me sick!" March shot out. "Why can't you be as sensible as Vane, or some of the rest of us."

Vane laughed deprecatingly. "I'm not exactly composed, but I am rather keeping a grip on myself, at that. Well, I suggest we all get together in a group. That way, we'll know what the others are doing."

"When will we sleep?" inquired Lemley.

"When will we sleep?" Hagerstown took up the refrain, his voice going tremolo. "How will we know the ones who are awake won't be plotting the murder of those who are asleep? I tell you, I can't stand it! I'm going to sit right here and defend myself!"

"Oh, oh," said Wright. "There it starts."

"What starts?" That was Latham.

Wright was smirking. "Aristotle or some other Greek said that when a social group got above six they'd start breaking up into little cliques. What chance have we got when our sociable little group starts breaking up?"

"Who's breaking away except Hagerstown?" said March fiercely.

"You think *I'm* going to trust myself to a pack of wolves? No, *thank* you. I'll stay here, and wait for you guys to bump yourselves off."

"That goes for me, too," said Lemley, who seemed, in his own callous way, to be enjoying the situation. "Leave your radios on, fellows. I'd like to know which one goes first."

"And who does the job, of course," smirked Wright.

The silence was clammy. Vane found himself breathing abnormally fast. When he spoke, his voice was hoarse.

"You, March, Latham, myself—we'll get together, and talk this over."

"All right," said Latham, his voice hard as steel.

March agreed, and without paying any attention to the three others, they talked the matter over. It was quite easy to believe that the merest jump would carry them from side to side of the planet, traveling at any angle. Latham suddenly remembered that Newton had once dealt with the theoretical problem; had proved that at all points on the interior of a hollow planet, the forces of gravitation canceled out. So if this planet was theoretically perfect in its hollowness—that is, practically homogenous, and with practically equal diameters in all directions—then the thing would work.

Talking it out, they discovered it would not do to meet at the center of the planet. They'd miss each other, inevitably, since inequalities on the surface would cause them to deviate from the vertical; and since their velocities, arising entirely from the speed with which they jumped, would certainly not be uniform.

"We'll meet at a point where one of us happens to be, then," decided Latham. "Agreeable? All right. As I see it, all six of us are on the interior equator. The order runs: myself, Lemley, March, Wright, Vane, Hagerstown. We're spaced equally."

"Which gives us the same chance, like runners at the start of a race," said Vane gloomily. "The two cliques are mixed together, too. Notice that?"

"By Heaven," snarled March, "if I ever get out of this—"

Latham heaved a sigh of resignation. "Keep cool, March. Vane, I guess you're our destination. The three of us form a triangle, the two legs equal in length. March and I are at the ends of the base line. So if March and I take the jump, we'll land at about the same time."

"The point is," said March, "how fast can a man jump?"

"Look at it this way. We don't have to overcome gravity, only our own inertia. We can assume it takes a high jumper about a second to jump six feet. The acceleration rate on Earth is thirty-two feet, isn't it? That is, at the end of a second, a freely falling body is falling at that speed. Then our athlete not only jumps six feet, but jumps fast enough to overcome that thirty-two feet. Although none of us are athletes—far from it—we ought to be able to make around thirty-four, or thirty-six feet.

True? Get set, then, March. Watch your chronometer, and we'll figure our actual speed later on. Get set, go!"

Latham flexed his powerful legs, and shot himself up from the hard, unyielding surface of the planet at an angle determined by Vane's carrier wave.

The record for the high jump, he thought cynically.

He had his head turned toward the blackness above him. He noted now that somehow he had acquired a rotation, for he slowly turned until he saw the fluorescent surface beneath. It was like nothing so much as a huge bowl, with the sides steepening in an even curve. As he moved outward, at a speed he could not guess with any exactness yet, the rim of the bowl continued to extend outward, but grew fainter in the process. Within fifteen minutes, he could see only the faintest gleam of lavender luminiscence. Another five minutes took even that. Then, to all intents and purposes, he was suspended in a void of absolute blackness. He could, of course, feel no motion, since his speed was constant.

He got in touch with March, exchanged a few comments, and then told Vane to turn his carrier wave on after an hour or so, and switch it back in after that every five minutes or so.

"When we land," Latham explained, "we'll turn our sets on, and then you'll catch our wave. That way we'll find each other without wasting power."

"Hurry it up," said Vane dispiritedly. "This is the first time in years I haven't had somebody around to keep me company. Don't be surprised if you find a raving lunatic. I've got plenty of time to brood about my past sins."

His guffaw almost split Latham's eardrums. He turned off his reciver in disgust. Vane, in Latham's opinion, was an egotistical fool, though at times he seemed to have a

187

level head. The Voice—damnation, what could you call the fellow?—had had Vane down to a T. And for that matter, he'd also had friend Latham down to a T.

Latham scowled to himself. There was something unbearably senseless about this whole thing. They were all fools, everyone of them. Planning some way out of this mess. Good God, couldn't they see there wasn't any way out?

Even Lemley, Hagerstown, and Wright were fools. Going to sit and wait until the others killed each other off, were they? Why didn't they get up and *do* something?

Latham's gloved hand dropped to the hilt of his sword. His lips twisted in grim humor. "Why," he asked himself, "don't I do something?" He pulled out the sword, for amusement slashing it back and forth. It was an épée, no good for slashing, but an excellent weapon for piercing a man's body.

Suddenly, a thought came to him, and he turned on his receiver. He received two carrier tones. Whose were they? He was about to use his transmitter, when one went off. But he spoke anyway. The tone sounded like Vane's.

"That you, Vane?" he said sharply.

"Huh? No, this's me." Lemley's voice was unexpectedly genial. "I just had my picker-upper on to see if I couldn't snatch up a bit of conversation. This is the damnedest place. Ghostly. You know what I mean?"

"It's worse out here," said Latham. "Dark."

"I guess so. I feel all washed out. Tired. Notice nobody ele's got their receivers open. Maybe"—a harsh laugh crept into his voice—"maybe they're out visiting."

"Maybe," said Latham cryptically. He was about to sign off without another word when he thought to himself, *Why do that? Lemley isn't so bad, though he's got the moral sense of a turtle.* To Lemley he said, "I'll get in touch with you again."

"OK," Lemley said, yawning.

By the chronometer above Latham's eyes, he timed his trip across as something more than four and a half hours. During that time, he got hungry and thirsty. Without thinking about it, he swung his food kit around, drew out the water tube, and sucked water—just one mouthful. Then he stopped, frowning.

"Five days," he mused to himself. For the first time the real situation hit him. He let the water tube roll back into the food kit. "I'm not hungry, after all," he mused, and frowned.

The first suggestion of light came, and grew in intensity, until the violet-tinged "bowl" took shape. He was rotating, now. He didn't feel like landing on his head, particularly at this velocity. At the last moment he managed to twist around so that his body was parallel to the surface. Thus he struck on his hands and feet. He had already switched current into his shoes, and thus was held fast with no danger of a rebound. He stood up, and reflecting that he had not been able to contact Vane once in the hours he had been floating, switched on his headset. Three carrier waves came in. One belonged to Wright, another to March, another to Lemley. Both Hagerstown and Vane were missing.

Wright, the food distributor, was suspicious. "You and March are too damned near, Latham. I'm warning you to keep away. I'm not being ganged up on by anybody."

"Where's Vane?" rumbled March. "I couldn't contact him on the way down."

"How long have you been down?" demanded Latham.

"Well, it took me about four hours and twenty minutes."

"I managed it in twenty minutes more than that. You've been here longer than I have. Are you *certain* you haven't heard Vane—or seen him?" Latham's voice was ugly.

"I said I didn't!" March blazed. "Keep your insinuations to yourself. I'll try again."

But Vane's carrier wave did not show up.

A grim smile played around Latham's hard lips. Was Vane the type that would hunt up another man with malice aforethought? Else, why would his carrier wave be off? Or was he—dead? Either dead or roaming, that was certain.

March and Latham finally agreed to work their ways toward each other. Latham pulled up one of the collapsible screens on his helmet, discovered it cut off part of March's waves, thus knew that March was in that direction. March's wave strengthened as he moved.

Coincidentally, Wright's also loudened.

"I'm warning you!" Wright shot out. "If you fellows try to hem me in, I'll jump, straight up!"

"Oh," Latham said, carelessly, "don't forget we've got six-shooters." He smiled.

"You're threatening me!" Wright panted. "You hear that, Lemley? You hear that? If my wave is suddenly cut off, you'll know who did it."

The chain-store owner yawned. "That," he said, "would be a shame."

"You needn't be such a fool," growled March.

Latham said patiently, "What I'm wondering is how we happened to land so near Wright, March. Didn't we start out for Vane?"

"It's a screwy setup." Lemley yawned.

March suddenly came out of the gloom, and as he saw Latham rushed toward him, in a pure gesture of relief.

Latham's lips hardened, and he stepped back, and pulled his six-shooter from his waist. He was a capable shot.

"One step nearer, March," he said coldly, "and you get it in the belly."

March gaped. His hands flew up and clasped his helmeted head. He groaned. "My God, Latham. You're crazy; we're all crazy! You thought *I* was coming after *you?* I was relieved, that's all—relieved!" He seemed unable to comprehend it.

Latham remained cold. "Perhaps it was a gesture of friendship. I really wouldn't know. At any rate, I'd suggest that neither of us make any sudden motions."

March agreed limply, still shaking his head. "Well, here we are," he said wearily. "So what?"

"Let's see if our sacred lineup is preserved."

Lemley, for some reason, had switched off. Latham made repeated calls before he came in again. Hagerstown answered, then Wright.

Vane was missing.

The order was somewhat mixed up due to March's and Latham's movements, but the three others were in their correct places. That meant then, that instead of landing in what might have been termed Vane's sector, March and Latham had landed in Wright's.

Latham thought about this for a while, and then thought of something which began to bring some sort of order out of the chaos. His capable jaw set, and he made a motion to March to switch off his radio entirely; Latham did the same, and then beckoned March. But March was suspicious and made vigorous denials. Impatiently, Latham put his arms above his head. March nodded energetically and did the same, and then approached. Latham maneuvered until their helmets were touching.

"Can you hear me?"

"Just about," March nodded in surprise.

"The sound is carried through the helmets. Now listen. Did you ever stop to think that our Nemesis told us this planet was rotating?"

The railroad magnate frowned. "Y-yes."

"While we were floating across the planet toward Vane, the planet was carrying Vane away from us, and putting Wright in his place. So that's where we landed."

March jerked his head up and stared at Latham. "Good God!"

Latham smiled twistedly. "Now what if there was a master mind among us who thought of that before we did? And put it to some use and got Vane out of the way, afterward figuring out where he *should* be, and jumping there?"

"How do you know Vane's out of the way?" March's voice was shaken.

"Well," Latham conceded, "he might be jumping around at that, with his own plan in his head. In that case, all of us are still alive, aren't we?" His lips twisted again. His gray eyes lidded. "You know," he suggested, "it'd be much better if Vane was dead."

March nodded, his eyes staring. "I know," he said huskily. "The food supply would begin to localize."

For a moment they drew their heads back and stared at each other with a series of new thoughts in their eyes.

"I'm hungry now," the railroad magnate said bluntly. "But I'm afraid to eat. Haven't got the nerve."

"Of course. But if Vane's dead, there's one man at least who's got ten-days' food supply. If he's not too sick to eat." He added slowly, "Maybe we better find out who killed Vane—or if he is dead."

"How?"

"We'll go where Vane should be," said Latham.

He stooped over and with the sharp metal tips of his gloves drew a circle on the metallic surface of the planet, and marked six dots, spaced equally, on the rim of the circle. He studied it for a moment. Then he straightened up.

"While we were crossing the planet," he mused, "the planet rotated one sixth. Wright's position moved where Vane's was. Vane's moved where Hagerstown's was. Hagerstown's where mine used to be. Mine where Lemley's was. Lemley's where yours used to be. So by setting our course toward where Hagerstown is *now*, we'll land where Vane *will* be."

March nodded doubtfully.

Latham found Hagerstown's carrier wave, and by careful rotation of his antenna, and setting of his screens, found the exact course.

"Hard business, this," muttered March. "Jumping at an angle."

They set themselves, swayed to the correct angle, cut the circuit to their shoes, and pushed themselves out.

Latham watched his chronometer, and when four hours was up, placed his binoculars to his eyes, and waited for the first sign of light. In a few minutes, it came. Latham swept the binoculars over the territory he could see. The land below was a huge bowl, fluorescing, and was, on the whole, smooth. Latham suspected he should see Vane, if the man were anywhere in that area.

March, who had one arm hooked through Latham's, sighted Vane first. Or at least they supposed it was Vane.

"He's standing up," said March. "I guess he's alive."

"Why should he fall down?"

They landed safely, perhaps a mile from the figure, and started immediately in that direction, and finally reached the standing figure, which proved to be that of Andreas Vane, after all.

And he was truly dead, a sword having evidently been plunged through his spacesuit, into his back. There was a jagged gash in the suit where the air had rushed out. Vane had died mostly from the sword thrust, but partly from asphyxiation. His face was purple, and his swollen, bloody tongue was protruding from his mouth. His food kit was empty, both of water and of food.

"*I* couldn't have done it," said March, staring at Vane without repugnance.

"Of course not," Latham conceded. He did not bother to make a denial himself. He stood swaying on his magnetic shoes, thinking.

March looked at him queerly. "I think Hagerstown did it."

Latham raised his eyebrows.

March went on, still looking at Latham significantly. "All Hagerstown had to do was to know that the planet rotated—or to remember it, rather. He remembered that and made his plans accordingly. Also, Vane's sector was right next to Hagerstown's, and was rotating toward Hagerstown's. All Hagerstown had to do was to jump at a very low angle, just skim the surface of the planet and land where Vane was. Then find him."

"Vane would have fought back," mused Latham. "No, maybe he wouldn't. Nobody'd suspect Hagerstown of that."

"A cornered rat will fight harder than a free one."

"What do we do? I'd suggest we go after Hagerstown. The man's got a mind!" Latham exclaimed, in a burst of wonder. "He must have jumped all the way back to where he was supposed to be. By the time we had landed and found each other, he had plenty of time to jump back."

March's thick lips set, and his gloved hand fell to his

sword. His lips formed five words. "Let's go and get him."

Latham smiled quizzically. "To get even with him? To punish him? Or to get his food supply?"

"What does it matter?"

"This is leading up to one thing," said Latham.

"What?"

"Eventually, unless we have the good sense to separate, one of us is going to murder the other."

They found Hagerstown by the same process they had used on Vane. They came up on him from two directions. Hagerstown was standing upright, swaying slightly, his magnetic shoes holding him firm to the planet. March and Latham came up behind him, their headsets off. March threw Latham one fierce look, and then drew his sword, and was about to plunge it into Hagerstown's back, when Latham grasped his arm.

Latham's cynical lips formed the words, "Maybe he didn't do it, after all. He's asleep."

March's heavy face wrinkled as if he hadn't heard aright. With a half-angry motion he turned on his headset, and gestured to Latham. Latham shrugged and turned his set on.

"You're crazy!" March rasped. "Didn't we decide Hagerstown was guilty?"

"Lemley and Wright can hear us talking," suggested Latham.

"To hell with 'em! Didn't we?"

"I'm not sure now. Look." Again Latham drew a circle on the metal surface. "Lemley could have done it."

March said in a rage, "Lemley couldn't have done it! We were talking to him while we crossed."

"We were tumbling around in empty space. We couldn't have known where Lemley was. He could have jumped across to where he knew Vane would be. He could have murdered him, and then jumped back to where he was supposed to be. By the time he got back, the planet would have rotated two sixths."

March's shoulders sagged, and a pallor came to his face. "Then we don't know about anybody. By the same token, Wright could have done it!" His face was wild.

Latham studied him, his hard eyes half lifted. "You think we're not getting any place. Only one man gone."

March looked at Hagerstown's unprotected back and pointed. His finger was trembling. "What's the difference?" his lips said.

Latham nodded. "What *is* the difference?" he said, quizzically. Then, "Have you ever killed a man?"

March panted, "Certainly I did. Once."

"That tells me a lot. You don't mind making the confession, which means that you believe none of us—except one—will remain alive. If it's you, there's nobody to snitch. If it isn't you, it doesn't matter anyway."

"I never did believe that more than one would escape."

"But subconsciously you did. Now you don't. Which makes it a certainty. You're willing to murder Hagerstown."

March's eyes were bloodshot, and he was crouching like a beast. "Certainly I am," he snarled. "Why waste time? Why not get it over with?"

"By the same token, you're willing to murder me." Latham felt a peculiar boiling in his stomach. He had never been sick inside a spacesuit. He clenched his fists and did the only thing that seemed sensible. Bent his legs as far down as they would go, snapped off the current in his shoes and jumped.

And left March with his victim.

Latham still felt sick, but it was half in loathing of himself. He closed his eyes and knew he was trembling.

He was on his way an hour before he caught anybody's wave.

He listened to the babbling, horrified voice with an incredulity that turned to hysteria. His stomach began to heave, and he knew he was laughing. His own laughter was a hell inside his helmet. Tears began to run down his cheeks, and he doubled up in midspace, and felt as if he was being torn across the stomach, torn clear in two.

I'm crazy, he thought to himself. *And I thought I was strong. I'm a weakling. But God, I can't stop.*

But he did stop, eventually, gasping. Exhausted, he felt every muscle in his body relax; he drifted, trembling, and determinedly set his lips, forcing himself to breath evenly, to think logically.

After perhaps ten minutes, he said weakly, "Hagerstown."

Hagerstown spoke cautiously. "Is something wrong? You sounded as if you'd lost your mind."

"You," said Latham, and laughed again. He caught himself. "It's *you* that's wrong. You shouldn't be alive. March should have killed you. Did he—or didn't he?"

"That's what I started to tell you when you took the fit." Hagerstown's own voice had a suggestion of hysteria. "I must have been sleeping, but I woke up and turned around and he was coming at me with his sword. God! There was only one thing I could do. I shot him. He's dead." The food buyer's voice quavered. "If this keeps up, I'll go crazy," he said hoarsely.

"Where are you now?"

"Here. Where I've always been! Wasn't that the agreement?"

"I didn't know there was any agreement," said Latham wearily. He managed to think cynically again. "You took his food, of course."

"Somebody else besides March is dead," Hagerstown whispered.

"Sure. Vane. How did you know?" Latham snapped.

"There were two food rations in March's kit."

Latham groaned, and shut his eyes, his nerves beginning to ball up, March. March. *March!*

"Hagerstown," he said, "protect yourself. With three food rations, you're a worthy prize for anybody. Perhaps you'd better discontinue your pacific activities and do some scouting around yourself. I still don't see how March could have had time to do it." He groaned again.

"Nobody has his carrier wave on," Hagerstown protested in fright.

"They could have had their receiver on," Latham sighed. "Go to your own hell, Hagerstown. I'm on the way to mine." And he cut connections.

For a long time Latham drifted in a state of semicoma. Then the familiar sight of land brought him back to full consciousness. From force of habit, he took out his binoculars, and scanned the territory. No one down there —yet. As he approached the surface, of course, the surface rotated away under him. He kept the binoculars to his eyes, and suddenly stiffened. There were two figures down there. Only one was moving. Suddenly it stopped. Latham craned his eyes, but saw only that that figure had a gun in its hand. He heard nothing, but saw one of the figures drop. Without the waste of a second, the killer worked over the body swiftly, then stood upright. Suddenly it jumped, at an angle. Frantically, Latham trained the binoculars on it—but sight was lost in the darkness.

He knew one thing only: one of the figures had been

Wright, the other Lemley. A process of elimination would reveal the murderer. And Latham felt that he would have no qualms about killing a man who deliberately, and with aforesight, killed another person.

He landed awkwardly, and with some force, but struggled to his feet, and slid across the surface in the peculiar manner necessitated by magnetic shoes.

He dropped to one knee, and trained his flashlight on the face of the murdered man. The sightless eyes of Wright stared up at him. A bullet had evidently got him in the back, and death had come from a combination of asphyxia and bleeding. There was blood caked around Wright's mouth, frozen into crystals.

Lemley, then, had been the murderer. Latham came to his feet and stared up into the darkness.

He thought vaguely, *I must have the desire to kill. Anybody at all. But I haven't got the guts to kill without provocation. Lemley murdered Wright. Thus I have the provocation. I make myself believe I'm avenging Wright —when Wright wasn't worth avenging.*

No. I want Lemley's food supply. That will give me three rations and Hagerstown three rations. And Hagertown's a cinch!

His lips twisted again, and he stood there, waiting for Lemley's carrier wave.

It came in presently. "Anybody home?" said Lemley. "I'm picking up somebody. Have you committed murder yet, friend? I've heard it's the newest fad."

"Don't be funny," said Latham, coldly. "What are you doing?"

"Eating," said Lemley cheerfully. Smacking sounds came over the receiver. "But concentrates aren't very satisfying."

"Whose concentrates—yours or Wright's?"

THE MEN AND THE MIRROR

Latham's receiver was silent for a full ten seconds. Lemley laughed harshly.

"My own," he snapped; then he laughed more agreeably. "So I murdered Wright, did I, Latham? How many are left, by the way?"

"Myself, you, Hagerstown."

"How do you know I murdered Wright, Latham?" Lemley's voice was mocking. "Maybe it was Hagerstown."

"I saw you."

"Hm-m-m. Well, what's the difference? Whether I did, or you did, or Hagerstown did. It all comes out the same in the end. And even if I did murder him, what about it?"

Latham frowned and hesitated. Lemley wouldn't confess anything if the finger of God was on him. "Stay where you are," he growled. "I'll see what Hagerstown has to say."

Lemley snickered again. "Why bother about Hagerstown? OK, OK, I'll be here waiting." A sucking sound came from the receiver. "That's my own water," Lemley informed Latham, and broke connections.

But Latham already had his location. He set himself at the correct angle, and jumped; and once he was beyond the light, he knew a sense of desolation and aloneness; as if the juice of life had been pumped out of him, leaving his bones dry. Futility was in his mind. The utter uselessness of everything. If he could only drift like this, forever, just the bare glimmer of thought to keep him alive—like an amoeba.

He would have to kill Lemley. And then, as a matter of course, Hagerstown.

Again he was using his binoculars. And saw Lemley, standing upright, with his own binoculars up to his eyes, staring into blackness. He was looking directly at Latham.

"Damnation!" Latham said with a sudden wildness. He

drew his six-gun with a trembling hand and trained it downward. With the other hand, he turned on his headset.

Hagerstown's and Lemley's waves came through.

"Fine," said Lemley. "Here we are, all together. Have you committed your little murder yet, Hagerstown?"

"I had to," mumbled the food buyer in a broken voice. "It was either March or me."

"My, my"—Lemley clicked his tongue—"what an innocent little man. In a short while, Hagerstown, there will be only two—unless Latham has only thoughts of peace on his mind. Care to land and talk this over Latham? After that, we can murder each other at our leisure."

"Your gun is drawn," said Latham coldly.

"So's yours."

"I prefer to keep mine handy."

"So do I. Go ahead and land, though."

Latham managed to stabilize himself, and for once floated down feet first. He switched current into his shoes, hit with a jar, and stuck, swaying.

Lemley was not more than fifty feet distant, the metal parts of his suit reflecting the faint violet light. They eyed each other without speaking for several seconds.

"Why don't you shoot?" said Latham coldly.

"It happens that I'm not a murderer at heart. Why accuse me of Wright's murder? Why not Hagerstown?"

"Don't be absurd, Lemley." Latham's eyes narrowed, and his legs forked to take care of the gun's recoil. "Hagerstown couldn't possibly have arrived where Wright was before I did. Because I definitely left him behind."

"Well—so naturally, if Wright was left dead," Lemley mused, "then the murder was pinned on me." He was lost in thought. Latham saw him nod his head in confirmation of his thoughts. "Yes, Latham, I think I see how it was done now. Hagerstown is your man. Go peddle your peanuts somewhere else. After you finish off Hagerstown, come back here and we'll talk—"

"My God!" babbled Hagerstown. "You talk as if I'm just a pawn in a game. You, Lemley, accuse me of a murder you did yourself! I warn you," he panted, "if either of you comes near me, I'll fight! I'll shoot you like I shot March, and I mean it!" His breath came rackingly.

"Good act," said Lemley, offhand. "What about it, Latham? You want to go across and get—*damn* you!"

Latham's gloved finger released the trigger, and a hard smile stretched his lips as he saw Lemley stagger, and heard curses coming through his receiver. Lemley's face was wild with fury. Latham pulled the trigger again, disappointedly saw that he'd missed. Lemley didn't seem to be dying either.

Something exploded in his brain. A flare of brilliancy mushroomed up. He knew, with a shock of horror, that he was screaming, screaming unendingly. The brilliancy died. He caught a glimpse of a pale-violet world, with Lemley outlined against it. He was still screaming, but not so piercingly now. The pale-violet became paler, approached darkness, became darkness absolute. His screams stopped. He knew, with a burst of utter grief, that he was dying.

Lemley stood over him, his thin face set in a scowl. "Damn fool," he said, his voice cracking. "Damn fool!"

He stopped and extracted food and water from Latham's kit, and placed the supplies in his own.

He hadn't yet made a good start toward the food monopoly, for now—all told—he had the food supply of only two persons: himself and Latham.

Hagerstown must have cut connections in the excitement, and though Lemley listened for an hour his wave did not come through.

"Huh!" he grunted sourly. "Damned if I'll let him come and get me. I'll go hunting myself."

He only had a slight idea where Hagerstown was. He should be somewhere near where he had been originally. That was two sixths of the circumference of the planet away, in a direction opposite to the planet's rotation. Lemley took a guess and jumped at an angle, his guess being based on the position of Latham's dead body. Latham's head, as Lemley remembered it, had been lying "across the equator." The ears, therefore, pointed out the equatorial plane.

He didn't trouble to time himself, and was surprised when the first glimpse of light came through. Unhurriedly, he placed his binoculars to his eyes, and for the first time —since he had actually stayed in his place, and had done no jumping—he saw the effect caused by the gradual diminution of light. He scanned the huge bowl of light, and was disappointed when he saw no sign of Hagerstown.

Better luck next time, he thought. *Hell! How do you get down in one piece!* His eyes popped as he saw the surface rushing up at him. He threw his arms back, and his feet came down. At the last minute, he remembered to bend his knees.

Lemley hit, and felt as if he were breaking himself off at the ankles. He had forgotten to send current through his shoes, and when he got his bearings again he discovered, in dismay, that he had bounced up from the surface of the planet, and was slowly—very slowly— drifting away. He squirmed around vainly, trying to throw himself back the mere two or three feet between him and a solid surface. He continued to move upward at a slow, steady rate—perhaps no more than a foot a second.

He ground out a curse of exasperation, and regarded the receding surface in perplexity. He frowned.

"OK," he said slowly. He blithely switched on his headset.

"Hagerstown," he snapped. No answer. He tried again and again, over a period of five minutes. His calculating eyes sparkled. He swore audibly, and ended with a groan of pain; not too loud, not too soft, but exactly the right note.

Then he snapped off his headset, and waited, as he slowly drifted upward, so slowly that after two hours the huge bowl was still plainly visible.

At the end of three hours, he was using his binoculars, anxiously. What he was waiting for came abruptly. A tiny speck, just large enough to be discerned, suddenly showed up where the rim of the bowl faded out into blackness. It was moving, silhouetted against the violet light. Lemley's breath broke loose and, exultantly, he waited until Hagerstown—for it was he—landed. Then he pulled the Colt, lined himself up, and fired.

The recoil sent him into tremendous velocity, and started him tumbling head over heels. He deliberately stiffened himself at full length, and by thrashing about with legs and arms stabilized himself again, with only a slight rotation. The bowl was approaching swiftly, and the dot that was Hagerstown was growing in size. Lemley held the gun in front of him, his lips drawn back over his teeth.

"Here's where you get yours!"

Closer, closer, Hagerstown was standing with his hands on his hips. Evidently he had thought to find a badly wounded man. Lemley was almost on top of him when Hagerstown looked up. A look of wild alarm crossed his face.

Lemley pulled the trigger.

"You're dead!" he yelled with the full power of his lungs. "You're dead! Fall down, damn you!"

Hagerstown did not fall down. His lips were open in a snarl of pure hatred and fright. He pulled his gun and blasted away at Lemley. He crouched, and shot no less than three times. Lemley wildly shot again. He was hanging then without motion, but this second shot sent him spinning back again, away from the surface.

Wildly, he pulled the trigger once more, aiming as best he might. He yelled furiously when he saw that Hagerstown was still standing; though naturally, he remembered, he couldn't fall.

Then he couldn't fire anymore. Partly because of the distance, mostly because he had only two bullets left, and he knew he'd need them to cut his velocity down.

His arm dropped, and in abject disappointment, he watched Hagerstown recede. The man was still standing. But—his arms suddenly dropped to his side, and his knees buckled. Lemley excitedly put the binoculars to his eyes, but all he could see was Hagerstown as a small receding dot. Lemley could not know if he was dead.

He must have crossed the planet in less than an hour. When land showed up, he fired at the land, twice. His formerly furious speed was cut to a slow drift. But within twenty minutes he had landed.

His gun was empty, but, nevertheless, his brow furrowed, he figured where Hagerstown should be; and so jumped. His angle was only slightly off, but he had to walk for two miles.

Hagerstown was dead, standing up, blood frozen around his nostrils.

In his food kit were the food rations of four people, all told: his own, Vane's, March's, and Wright's.

"What a shame!" said Lemley, mockingly. "The prime

devil of us all. So March murdered Vane? Not at all, although it might have been possible. You murdered Vane and told Latham that March had had two rations in his kit. You also murdered Wright, and must have used at least six bullets in order to get there before Latham, who thought you were me. But *I* murdered *you*. So laugh that off, cry baby!"

So, since Lemley had cornered the food supply successfully, his was a soft life for five weeks—within limits. On the food and water question he had to discipline himself rigorously. "It's only a habit, anyway," he told himself philosophically.

For amusement he jumped, using five dead bodies as his landmarks. He became so proficient in this art that once he made a perfect bull's-eye and landed square on March's spacesuited chest—from a point clear on the opposite side of the planet.

Once—although ammunition was limited—he made a flight across a diameter of the planet in a little more than thirty minutes. It cost him ten bullets.

He lost count of time, but knew, by the amount of food and water remaining, the approximate number of days that passed.

The last of his food went. One day later, he was forced to drink the last of his water.

He waited ten hours, his nerves tensed. Finally he snapped on his headset. "Voice," he snapped, "the famine's on. The population is about to die out."

The hands of the chronometer had gone around once more, and Lemley's tongue was beginning to swell, when a carrier wave sounded, and the Voice spoke, amusedly.

"The famine's over, Lemley." It spoke no more, though

Lemley swore thickly. Lemley stayed awake until he couldn't hold his eyes open; and then slept.

When he awoke, he was in a little cell, lying on a bed, wearing his ordinary suit. He jumped to his feet, stood looking around him, cautiously. Before him was a table, not heavily laden, but with enough to feed him twice over. He ate—and drank—and when he had finished, sat down on the bed and started to demand explanations.

He never got them. There was a puff of light, and a sickening odor assailed his nostrils.

Oh damn, he thought, and lost consciousness.

The plump man with the scarred face stopped for the first time since he had begun the story. He gestured to a waiter who had been impatiently staring at our table. He ordered a drink and raised his colorless eyebrows at me.

"I don't feel like drinking," I said, although my throat was dry. "I'm not hungry either," I said at the waiter. The waiter went away.

I forced my eyes back to those of the plump man.

"Go on."

"That's really all of the story. Lemley won out. Perhaps he should have. The debonair shall inherit the Earth."

"I thought it was 'The meek shall inherit the Earth.'"

"Some Biblical students claim that was the result of a bad translation. I prefer 'debonair.' At any rate, the word conveniently applies to Lemley. One of his characteristics is that he seldom took anything seriously. He was easygoing."

There was a hardness behind his genial blue eyes. "I'll say this much for Lemley. He woke up on Earth, after his strange experience, and did some serious thinking. The result of that was that he broke his chain stores up into a hundred small companies and sold them to individual buyers. He's had nothing to do with food since—in a commercial way, of course. He's fairly respected in some quarters now. I might say he's a new edition of himself— though the pages are becoming somewhat tattered again."

"Where'd you get the story?"

"Does it really matter?" He stared at me intently, his eyes acquiring a certain paleness. Before I knew what he was doing, he was on his feet, still staring at me.

"But I think you know the moral."

And then he was gone.

Slowly the soft music and laughing couples of the Sky Garden reached my mind again. I paid my check and left, and went to a private phone booth.

Jafee's voice answered presently. "Oh, you, chief." He seemed disgusted.

"I want you," I told him, "to draw up a report of the various complaints made by the employees of Venusian Metals."

"What good will that do?" he said sarcastically.

"Plenty. I've recently had a change of heart. Sure, voluntary. And there won't be a wage cut. I might actually manage an increase, instead."

"For heaven's sake," Jafee said in an awed tone.

"Change the letterheads and envelopes. Take your name off. Put mine on. Since I've decided to change my ways, I might as well come out in the open.

"D. Lemley, president—D. Lemley— Hell, does it sound that bad?" He had been choking.

" 'Scuse me, chief," he said apologetically. I could almost hear him scratching his head. Finally he admitted, "It's just that I can't understand what got into you, all of sudden."